BRING THE BOYS HOME

Bonnets and Bugles Series   10

BRING THE BOYS HOME

GILBERT MORRIS

MOODY PRESS
CHICAGO

ISBN: 0-8024-0920-2

5 7 9 10 8 6 4 2

Printed in the United States of America

To Jarred McCauley

I hope you become a great writer, Jarred,
and that with every word you write
you will glorify the Lord.

Contents

1
The Net Closes

Corporal Majors!"

Jeff stopped abruptly as a harsh voice came across the frozen air. He turned slowly, guiltily. As he expected, he saw his father, the colonel, standing outside his tent, glaring at him.

Jeff snapped to attention and brought his right hand up to a salute, touching the forage cap as he had been taught. He had been a drummer boy for two years in the Stonewall Brigade, but now at seventeen had been mustered into the regular service and appointed a corporal.

"Yes, Colonel," he said. His lips were so cold that he found it difficult to speak. He brought his hand down, knowing he was in big trouble.

Col. Nelson Majors walked up to his soldier son. They looked alike, these two. They had the same coal-black hair and black eyes. Jeff was fully as tall as his father, though much slimmer.

"Where have you been, Corporal?"

After a slight hesitation, Jeff said, "Into Richmond, sir."

"How many times does that make that you've been to Richmond in the last week?"

"Three times, Colonel."

"Well, that's about three times too many!"

Nelson Majors was ordinarily a soft-spoken man, but today his face was drawn with tension.

The siege of Petersburg had drained all the energy out of him. He had been wounded at the beginning of the siege and had not gotten his full strength back. He held himself up straight and said sternly, "Corporal, just because you're the son of the commanding officer doesn't give you any special privileges! I thought I'd made that clear to both you and your brother!"

"I'm sorry, sir." Jeff had no excuse. He had gotten permission from his lieutenant to go to town, but he knew that he had taken a shortcut. He was well aware that his father was never one to permit one of his sons to merit special attention, and now he made no defense.

"You can stand guard for an extra watch, Corporal Majors."

"Yes, sir."

Jeff returned his father's angry salute, and when the colonel ducked back inside the tent, he made his way down through the camp to the front lines.

Here were trenches protected by large logs and anything else that would stop a musket ball. They were not quite deep enough for a man to walk upright, so Jeff kept his head down. As he wound through the fortifications, from time to time he heard the explosion of a musket and the screaming of a minié ball as it split the air. Both sides were firing, and their trenches were less than two hundred feet apart in places.

A mortar exploded somewhere behind the lines, and he dropped down flat. When the dirt settled, he got up and continued his journey, finally arriving at the location where his squad was detailed to hold off the Yankees.

"Hello, Jeff. You bring anything good back to eat?"

Sgt. Tom Majors, Jeff's older brother, was sitting on a cracker box. He'd been talking to Charlie Bowers, the undersized drummer boy who had entered the service the same time as Jeff but was one year younger.

"Well, yes, I did," Jeff muttered. He flung down the bag. "There! You can have it!"

Charlie stared at him with his wide blue eyes. "What's the matter, Jeff? You look all put out."

"Pa—I mean the colonel—just bawled me out for going into Richmond."

"You had permission, didn't you?" Tom asked as he picked up the bag.

"Sure, I did. From the lieutenant. But that wasn't good enough."

Tom was barely listening. He had opened the bag and was pulling out its contents. "Cookies!" he said. "My, I haven't seen a cookie in years, it seems like!"

Jeff, however, was not thinking of cookies. "I don't see why he has to pick on me! What difference does it make whether I'm here or not?" he grumbled. He plopped himself down on a log that formed a part of the fortification and watched as the other two soldiers eagerly went through the rations. He refused the cookies. He had filled up on cookies when in Richmond.

Charlie said, "I think you're crazy, Jeff—turning down cookies just because you're upset with your pa."

Tom was munching happily, making a chocolate cookie last as long as he could. Then he said, "You

11

know Pa's pretty tense, Jeff. He's got a lot of responsibility here."

"That's right," Charlie said. "We're trying to hold too much of the line. Spread out all thin-like. Why, if the Yankees made a run at us, I don't know if we could hold 'em or not."

Jeff knew that both were right, and it was not his father's fault.

"Well," he muttered, "I guess it was worth it. Leah and I cooked up all this stuff, and I ate all I could so the rest of you could have what I brought back. But food's getting so scarce there that they couldn't give us much."

"Seems they found a chicken anyhow." Tom bit down on a fried chicken leg. "It beats anything we've had here lately."

The three soldiers were tired and dirty. A siege was a nasty sort of way to run a war, Jeff thought. There was no glory in it—no flags flying, no bands playing—just day after day risking death every time a man raised his head.

"The net's closing in," Tom said, glancing toward the Federal fortifications. "General Grant is getting more reinforcements all the time, and we're getting thinner. There's only one end to that."

Jeff nodded. "I reckon you're right, Tom. And Pa's got too much to do. I shouldn't have gotten sore at him like that."

Colonel Majors had been fortunate enough to commandeer a horse that would hold his weight. He was in Richmond, on his way home for the first time in days.

"Come on, boy. You can make it just a little farther." He urged the weary animal down the street.

12

Richmond was a pitiful sight, he thought. The mortars and the big guns of the Federals had arched over their deadly missiles, blowing large chunks out of the city.

He rode through the heart of town and saw that little was left of the daily life he remembered. When he'd first come here from Kentucky to join the Confederacy, Richmond had been a busy, prosperous city. Now, only a remnant was left of all of that. He saw bombed-out buildings, burned houses, holes in the street big enough to hide a horse. And he saw little hope in the eyes of those who were still trying to keep the Confederate war machine going.

Finally he reached home, a small, white frame house, which so far had been spared the destruction of the inner city. He slid off the bony animal, slapped him with some affection, and said, "You did a good job, boy. I'll see if I can find you some fodder." He tied the horse to the hitching post, then opened the door and called out, "Hey, where's my welcoming committee?"

Instantly he heard a child's voice, and then a blonde girl, no more than three years of age, came like a whirlwind. She hit him full force, and he laughed, picking her up and holding her high in the air.

"Well, here's my Esther!" He kissed her rosy cheek. His wife had died bringing Esther into the world, and for most of her life the child had been in the care of Dan and Mary Carter in Kentucky. Now, however, she was here to stay, and she had a new mother.

"Nelson, you're home!"

Eileen Fremont Majors greeted him with almost as much vigor as the child. At twenty-nine, she had brilliant red hair, green eyes, and, he knew, a great love for her new husband.

Nelson kissed her and then said, "You smell better than anything I've smelled in the last three weeks!"

Eileen ran her hand through his hair. "I'm glad you're here, dear. Come on. I know you're hungry. I'll fix you something to eat."

He followed her into the kitchen, noted the pleasant warmth of the wood stove, and sat down, saying, "I wish I could carry that stove back to the front lines with me."

"I'm afraid we don't have much to cook on it, but the fire's nice."

"How's the firewood holding out?"

"We'll manage."

Eileen busied herself making a meal, and soon it was set before him. "Only two eggs," she said, "but we got a piece of bacon yesterday, and here are some biscuits that I made this morning."

As her husband ate, Eileen sat beside him. Esther demanded her father's attention, and he pulled her up onto his lap and began to tell her stories, which she loved. After a time, however, he said, "Now, you let Daddy have a little time with Mommy, all right?"

"Will you tell me more stories after you talk to her?"

"Sure I will, sweetheart." He kissed her firmly, and she toddled off happily to play. "Where's Leah?" he asked.

"Oh, she's out fishing again."

"In this weather? She'll freeze to death!"

"She doesn't seem to mind, and the fish come in handy. Until the water freezes over, she says she'll keep at it. We'll have fish for supper."

Then Eileen plumped herself down in her husband's lap. "There," she said. "I've missed this lap of yours."

"I've missed having you in it." He stroked her hair. "I've missed you more than I should. I couldn't keep my mind on my business."

Eileen hesitated, then said, "I've got some more business for you to think about."

"What's that?"

"How would you feel if you had to buy another plate for the table?"

For a moment Nelson could not understand what she meant. He saw that she seemed somewhat apprehensive. And then the meaning of her question came to him. His black eyebrows went up with astonishment. "You don't mean that we're going to have a baby?"

"Yes! That's the business at hand." Eileen looked at him carefully and then said, "I hope you don't mind, Nelson."

"Mind? Why would I mind? I think it's wonderful!"

She obviously had been concerned about how he would take the news. Life during wartime was hard enough without any complications. She seemed to desperately need his assurance. "I'm so glad," she whispered. "I was afraid you wouldn't like it."

"Of course I like it, and don't you worry a bit. We'll make out fine."

Eileen whispered, "I hope it'll be a boy. That would be good, wouldn't it?"

"That would be very good!"

The dead of winter had not stopped the Yankee determination to take Richmond. Gen. Ulysses S.

15

Grant kept Lee and his Army of Northern Virginia off balance constantly. Lincoln had been reelected, General Sherman had captured Atlanta, and Savannah had surrendered. Now Sherman was on his way north to join Grant in a full-scale attempt to seize Richmond, which would end the war.

Even the promise of spring's coming could bring no hope to Lee's men. They were freezing and starving daily. Death, disease, and desertion slowly destroyed the once proud Army of Northern Virginia. In one five-week period, more than three thousand men simply walked off to go home and did not return.

General Lee knew that the biggest problem that winter was food. He said, "Unless the men and animals can be fed, the army cannot be held together and our present lines must be abandoned."

Colonel Majors was one of the officers called to a special staff meeting one day, and he saw that General Lee looked tired and worn. *He's become an old man!* Nelson thought with some astonishment. *This war is killing him!*

General Lee was indeed worn out and was suffering from the heart condition that would eventually kill him. However, there was always a dignity in the man, and as he explained to his officers how grim the situation was, that inherent strength that had kept the Army of Northern Virginia intact was still there.

"I must inform you gentlemen that our plight is severe," he said quietly. "As you must know, the Federals are increasing their strength daily while we are growing weaker with each hour."

"We can hold out, General," one of the officers spoke up at once.

"I pray so, but we must face reality." He went on to speak about the lines that had been cut and about the lack of food and ammunition.

When he dismissed the men, Nelson slowly walked back to his own sector, where he found Tom waiting.

"What did the general say, Colonel?" Tom was still learning to adapt to the use of an artificial limb. After losing a leg at Gettysburg, he had been mustered back into the service as a courier. It was intended that he would serve on horseback, but now he was in the trenches with the rest of the men.

His father frowned. "I've never seen General Lee like this. He's always been such a tower of strength, but now it seems that he has lost hope."

"If *he's* lost hope," Tom said, "I don't think the rest of us can do much better."

The colonel felt the biting air cut through his uniform. "I don't think so either. It's just a matter of time, Tom. We've got to realize that."

Tom rubbed his hands to warm them. His thoughts seemed far away.

Finally his father said, "I could guess what you're thinking."

Tom looked up and smiled guiltily. "Are you a mind reader now, Colonel?"

"I know my boys pretty well. You're thinking about Sarah."

Tom bowed his head. He and Sarah were practically engaged, but she was back in Kentucky and he was here in the frozen trenches—and he had been maimed by the war. "I still don't reckon Sarah would want a one-legged man, Pa."

"Don't be foolish, son!" Nelson said. "A leg is not a man!" But he knew Tom had not fully gotten over

17

the loss of the leg. His older son had always been strong and athletic and now felt he was not the man he'd been.

Tom looked out over the fortifications, thinking. Slowly he turned back to his father, saluted, and then limped toward the trenches to take his place in the line.

The colonel watched him go and thought, *That boy's hurting—and he's wrong about Sarah. But I guess every man has to learn to get along with his own handicaps.*

He walked away, wondering how to make the food go a little farther, how to make the lines stretch a little longer, and how to keep the Yankees at bay for just one more day.

2
Jeff Goes to Richmond

A hard freeze had transformed the clothes that Leah hung out earlier in the day. They had been soft and fluffy from the washing she'd given them in the iron pot, but now they were frozen stiff. As she approached the line, she muttered, "I should've known that this would happen!" But then she shrugged and began to take them down.

At sixteen, Leah had probably reached her full growth. She still saw herself as tall and gawky, but lately young womanhood had sculptured her into a more graceful figure. Her green eyes caught the light of the noon sun, and her blonde hair escaped from the woolen stocking cap that she had pulled down tightly.

Unpinning a suit of men's long underwear, she held it up for a moment. She grinned, bent the frozen garment in the middle, and began waltzing around with it, humming a song.

Then abruptly she halted. "This is *not* going to get the work done!" She gathered up as many of the stiffened clothes as she could and went back into the small frame house, set only twenty feet from the Richmond street.

A black-and-white cat met her as she entered the back door. He stared at the frozen long underwear. Then suddenly he made a jump. He dug his claws into the garment and bit at it fiercely.

"Cap'n Brown, you stop that!"

Leah picked up the cat and nuzzled him. "You'll have to behave yourself. These are just underwear—they're not going to hurt you." Holding the cat under one arm, she crossed the kitchen to the hall-way and made her way to a large bedroom, where she leaned the long johns against the wall. "Now you stay there," she admonished them, "and I'll go get the rest of you!"

After several trips, Leah had the room filled with frozen clothes. When she had them lined them up, waiting for them to thaw, she began preaching at them. "Now," she said, "listen to what I have to say. You're all good Confederate underwear, so I want you to behave yourselves like good Confederates. Do you hear me?"

"What in the world are you doing?"

Leah whirled, feeling red coming to her cheeks. "Oh, nothing, Eileen!"

"Did I hear you talking to those clothes?" Eileen asked curiously. But she smiled, and a dimple touched her cheek.

"I was just having a little fun." Leah picked up a petticoat. "See—they're all stiff as boards."

"They're clean anyway. I'm glad for that." Eileen touched a shirtwaist that was beginning to lose its stiffness. "It's hard enough to wash in the summer-time, but in the winter it's terrible. I just hope the soap holds out."

"They didn't have any anywhere in town that I could find," Leah said. "All the stores are out of just about everything." She gave the older woman a close look and said, "Eileen, what'll we do when there's no more soap?"

"I don't know, Leah. I just don't know."

There was a tinge of hopelessness in Eileen's voice, and in that she was like most Southerners. The Army of Northern Virginia was now trapped in Richmond, encircled by 100,000 Union soldiers. Every day the ring grew tighter, and everyone knew that things could not go on much longer. The South would have to surrender.

Eileen bit her lip suddenly and dropped the shirtwaist. She went to a chair and sat down.

Leah looked at her with surprise and crossed to stand beside the chair. "What's wrong, Eileen? Don't you feel well?"

"Not really."

"What is it? I hope it's not something serious."

Eileen looked up with a smile. "I'm afraid it is."

"Not *smallpox?*" Leah gasped.

"No, not smallpox." Eileen was pale, but she managed another smile. "I'm going to have a baby, Leah."

"A baby? You don't mean it!"

"Yes, I do." She took Leah's hand and squeezed it. "It's an awful time for having a baby, isn't it? Here in the middle of a war with our side about to be demolished."

Seeing the trouble in Eileen's eyes, Leah leaned over and kissed her on the cheek, then gave her a quick hug. "I think it's a wonderful time to have a baby, and it'll be a beautiful baby too. It'll either be beautiful like you are or be handsome like his father. Either way, it will be wonderful."

That seemed to cheer Eileen. She got up, saying, "I'm all right now. I just seem to get a little dizzy from time to time. Come along, and we'll see what we've got for supper tonight."

The two women went into the kitchen, and as they began to put together a meal, Leah said quietly, "I get lonesome for home sometimes."

Home for Leah was Kentucky. It had been home for her family, the Carters, and for the Majors family too, until the war had separated them. Leah had brought Colonel Majors's little girl to Richmond, but now that he was married again she felt in the way.

She turned suddenly to Eileen. "I think I'd better be going home soon."

"Perhaps you should. Not that we're not glad to have you, but with the war going the way it is, it's not safe for you here."

There was a pause, and Leah had another thought. "But if you're going to have a baby, you'll probably need help."

"You can't stay around here for that long!" Eileen exclaimed.

"I can stay as long as you need help," Leah said. "Let's talk about it later."

Jeff mounted the skinny army horse and sat looking down at the animal's bony shoulders. "I think I'm about as able to carry you as you are me," he muttered.

But a horse was a horse. In Petersburg there were few animals—there was no feed for them. He had obtained this mount only because his father had put in a word with the quartermaster.

"Go on into Richmond and see if you can find anything for us to eat, Corporal," the colonel had said.

Jeff dug his heels into the bony sides of the horse, who obliged by moving forward at a slow walk. Jeff did not urge him. He knew that the animal was old and had not been well cared for. *I feel sorry for all the horses,* he thought.

Still, it was always good to get out of the trenches, for the stench of death was there and the constant danger of being killed. All morning Jeff rode quietly along the road until he reached the capital.

Richmond was depressing too, he thought. Most of the stores were closed, and what few factories were still running were manned by gaunt workers with gray faces. He found no food at all for sale—at least none that could be bought with Confederate money.

"If I had greenbacks, I could buy some, I bet," he said. Strangely, Union cash was more welcome in Richmond than its own currency. Confederate money was worth practically nothing. Jeff had his pockets stuffed full, but he knew that it would take a miracle to find anyone willing to trade good food for worthless paper.

Then he had an idea. He took a road leading out of town and came, after an hour's ride, to a large mansion sitting on the left side of the roadway. Kicking the horse with his heels, he muttered, "Come on, boy. It won't hurt to try here."

When he slipped off the horse, he was greeted by a grinning black man, who said, "Hello, Mr. Jeff! I haven't seen you lately."

"No, Zeno. Been in the trenches at Petersburg."

"Let me take that hoss. You go on in. Miss Lucy, she's here on the place."

"Thank you, Zeno."

Jeff ran up the steps, knocked on the door, and was met by one of the house servants, a small black girl that he knew. "Hello, Verbena. Is Miss Lucy here?"

"She sure is, Mr. Jeff. You come on in, and I'll fetch her for you."

Jeff waited in the foyer.

Lucy came, almost at once, and held out her hands. "Jeff!" She smiled up at him. "I'm so glad to see you!"

He took her hands and looked down at the small girl. Lucy Driscoll was one of the prettiest girls Jeff had ever seen. "Good to see you too, Lucy," he said. "How have you been?"

"Just fine. Come on back! Cecil is here." Her eyes twinkled for a moment, and she said roguishly, "But I forgot, officers and regulars don't mix, do they?"

"Not very well."

At that moment a young man wearing the uniform of a Confederate second lieutenant emerged from the drawing room. "Jeff! Good to see you!" Cecil Taylor, at seventeen, was thin as a rail. He had chestnut hair and bright blue eyes and a crooked grin. "I don't guess we have to worry about 'sirs' around here," he added.

The three young people went into the drawing room, where Lucy asked one of the servants to bring in cake and tea. She served it herself, asking Jeff, "How are things at Petersburg?"

"Not very good," Jeff said glumly. He glanced at Cecil. "I guess you know more about the whole picture than I do."

Shaking his head, Cecil said, "It's not the same thing. I've asked a hundred times to be put on active duty in the lines, but they won't let me go."

Jeff swallowed a piece of cake. "I wish they'd let us change jobs. You'd be welcome to mine."

"Aw, you don't mean that, Jeff."

Actually Jeff knew he didn't. He wanted to be with his unit, what was left of the Stonewall Brigade, and he well knew that he did not want to leave his father or his brother. Still, he also knew that Cecil felt bad about not getting in on the fighting, so he said, "Don't worry. Pretty soon you'll be at it. I think everybody will."

"I feel like a slacker," Cecil said.

"You're not that!" Lucy put a hand on Cecil's arm. "You have to do what your officers tell you. If they told you to fight, you'd fight in a minute."

Jeff noted with interest her sparkling eyes and that her fondness for Cecil showed in her face. He knew that Cecil had been in love with Leah, but after finding she didn't care for him, it would be natural enough for him to turn to Lucy Driscoll. The two had grown up together, and both were children of wealthy planters.

After a while Jeff admitted, "Actually, I've come begging. I don't suppose you've got anything to eat I could take back to some of my friends at the front."

"I'll bet we do!" Lucy jumped up. "Let me get on a coat, and we'll go see what we can find."

They actually filled a sack with an assortment of food. Jeff flung the bag over the horse's back and mounted behind it. Then he reached down and shook Lucy's hand. "You're making some Confederate soldiers mighty happy, Lucy." He smiled at her. "I thank you for all of them."

"Come back, Jeff, and don't get hurt," she said. "I wish I were going with you, Jeff."

"You stay here, Cecil. You take care of Lucy now."

Cecil looked at Lucy, and it seemed something passed between them. But then the lieutenant looked back at Jeff. "I sure wish I could do more than push papers around."

As Jeff slowly moved down the driveway on the skinny horse, he thought, *Those two are going to fall in love. I'm not much on romance, but I know it when I see it.*

"Jeff! You come in this house!"

Jeff had been standing on the step when Leah opened the door. He let her grab him by the arm and drag him inside.

"Esther," she called, "come and see your big brother!"

Three-year-old Esther came trotting in. She squealed with delight and ran for Jeff. He caught her up, tossed her high, and said, "How's my baby sister?"

"Jeff—Jeff! Come on, I'll show you my dolls!"

"All right. Let's see your dolls."

He sat on the floor as Esther named off her dolls, giving their family histories.

"She talks like a parrot, doesn't she?" Jeff said to Leah.

She sat on the floor with Jeff and his small sister. "Yes, she does. She's very bright."

At that moment Eileen came in. "Jeff! I didn't know you were here!"

Jeff scrambled to his feet, walked over to his stepmother, and gave her a hug and a kiss on the cheek. "Now, that's from your husband. He'll do better when he gets here."

"How is he, Jeff?"

"He's fine!" This was not exactly true, for nobody in the front lines at Petersburg was fine, but Jeff wanted to encourage her.

"Well, I'm going to fix you the best supper you ever had, and you can take some back to Nelson."

Jeff was glad that his father had found a companion. Though he had been opposed to their marriage at first, he really liked Eileen.

"I'll go chop wood for my supper," he said.

"Take me too," Esther said.

Finally, after much pleading, Leah bundled her up, and the three went outside. Jeff split the wood, enjoying that job as he always did, and they went in only when Eileen called that supper was ready.

It was indeed a good supper, better than he had had in some time. Eileen had managed to find a little beef and some vegetables, and Jeff wolfed down the food hungrily.

After the meal, he and Leah sat in the parlor playing with Esther. They had a moment alone when Eileen put Esther to bed.

"I just came from over at the Driscoll place," Jeff said.

Instantly a flush came to Leah's cheeks. "I still feel guilty about the way I treated Cecil—just trying to make you jealous. And I still have trouble forgiving myself for it."

Seeing her face, Jeff said quickly, "I know you feel bad about it—but I don't think you have to." He grinned broadly.

"I don't know why you'd say *that*."

"Because I think you would've made Cecil miserable if you had married him." His grin widened. "You're enough to drive a man crazy!"

"Well, I like that!"

"I honestly don't think you need to worry though. It looks to me like Cecil has his eye on Lucy."

After a moment, Leah nodded. "I hope so. They'd be perfect for each other. They've grown up together, and they know all about each other."

"I'm not sure *that's* a good idea," Jeff said, concealing a grin this time. "He'll know all her faults, and she'll know all of his."

"That's right," Leah said, and she punched him sharply. "And, therefore, there won't be any bad surprises."

"I just hope Cecil doesn't have to fight. This war's going to be over soon. He could get himself killed meantime."

"So could you!"

"Oh, I know, but I'm used to fighting. I've learned how to handle it, but Cecil's kind of fragile."

The next morning when Jeff left, Leah held up Esther for him to kiss.

The child grabbed his hair and held on tightly. "Don't go, Jeff!" she wailed.

"Got to go, sweetheart," Jeff whispered. Unexpectedly, he leaned past her and kissed Leah on the cheek. "Now, that's all the kisses you get for a while," he admonished her. He laughed at her indignation, then said, "Take care of everything here, Leah."

As the women and the little girl watched Jeff ride out on the scrawny horse, Leah said, "I wish he didn't have to go."

"I wish none of them had to go," Eileen said quietly.

3
The Last Battle

The Civil War had gone on for almost five years. Hundreds of thousands lay in graves all over the South, and others, crippled by the war, had gone back to their homes. If the war had been a play, the Battle of Petersburg marked what might be called the last act. The Confederates, starving and freezing in the filthy trenches, held grimly on. However, death, disease, and desertion continued.

General Lee informed the authorities in Richmond that the end was near. When he returned to camp, he told his son, "I have been up to see the Congress, and they do not seem to be able to do anything except eat peanuts and chew tobacco while my army is starving."

One Southern soldier wrote in that freezing January of 1865, "There are a good many of us who believe this shooting match has been carried on long enough. A government that has run out of rations can't expect to do much more fighting. . . . Our rations are all the way from a pint to a quart of cornmeal a day, and occasionally a piece of bacon large enough to grease your plate."

General Grant continued to push against the Confederates. Lee's line was now stretched more than thirty-seven miles, and he had only 35,000 men able to fight. Lee's only alternative was to evacuate Petersburg and Richmond and join Gen. Joseph Johnston in the Carolinas.

General Lee commanded Gen. John B. Gordon to attack, and Gordon decided to throw his strength against Fort Stedman, which lay near Grant's major supply line. Almost half of the Confederate forces were to be thrown into this attack, and at 4:00 A.M. on March 25, General Gordon gave the order to advance. It was to be the last concerted effort of the Confederates against the Union army.

Jeff looked up with surprise when Tom said, "Well, look who's here, Jeff."

Jeff got to his feet at once, for none other than Cecil Taylor was the subject of Tom's remark. The two stood and saluted Cecil, who, grinning broadly, returned their salutes.

"At ease, men," Cecil said. He was wearing a spotless gray uniform, which contrasted violently with the dirty, ragged dress of the two before him. "I'm glad to see you, Corporal," Cecil said. He winked, still grinning broadly. "I told you that I'd get down to where the real fighting is. I just pestered them until they finally would've done anything to get rid of me."

Jeff glanced at Tom and figured that they both had the same thought. *He just doesn't know what he's getting into—but he'll find out!*

Jeff said, "Was everything all right back home, sir?"

"You mean Leah and your family? Yes," Cecil said. "I made a point to go by and check on them. As a matter of fact, I brought letters for all of you." He rummaged in the letter pouch he wore suspended by a strap and came up with three pieces of folded paper. "No envelopes, and it looks like they had to use wallpaper, but at least they're letters."

"They sure are!" Jeff said, grabbing them greedily. "I'll take this one to Pa right away!"

"I'll just go along with you. I've been assigned to his command," Cecil said. "You can introduce me formally."

As the boys started toward headquarters, Jeff automatically hunched down. When a shell came screaming over, he reached up and, without apology, jerked Cecil down to a crouch. The two leaned against the dirt fortification as the exploding shell rained a shower of mud and debris down on their heads.

Cecil looked shocked. He brushed at the dirt that had fallen on his shoulders and tried to smile. "Well, that one missed us."

"Yes, sir, it did. Come along," Jeff said, "and keep your head down, sir."

Jeff led Cecil to his father's command post, where Colonel Majors's eyes opened wide when Jeff announced his companion's new assignment. "Well, we need all the help we can get. We lost the lieutenant of C Company yesterday. You can fill in for him, Lieutenant."

"You think we'll get to see some action?" Cecil asked eagerly.

Jeff grinned slightly, but the colonel kept a straight face. "I think there's a very good possibility of that. The main thing, Lieutenant, is to survive."

"Yes, sir, but do you think there'll be a charge against the Yankees?"

Colonel Nelson looked over to where the Union troops were firmly entrenched. The men over there had fresh uniforms, good food, plenty of guns and cannon, and there were plenty of them. "I hope not," he said. "We'll do well just to hang on here."

Jeff noted the disappointment on young Taylor's face.

His father said in kindly fashion, "I just want to see all my men get home alive, so take care of yourself."

Jeff went back to his post, where he found Tom waiting for him. "Did you give the letter to Pa?"

"I forgot all about it!" Jeff said, snapping his fingers with annoyance. "Well, I'll take it back after while. What do you think about Cecil?"

"I think you'd better stick close to him," Tom said. He was tired and dirty and needed a shave. Weariness had rimmed his eyes with dark circles, as it had most of the men. He slumped down on the ammunition box at his feet. "He's just too eager. He could get himself killed—and he could get some of the other men killed. You watch him close, Jeff."

The young lieutenant with the fresh uniform stuck out like a sore thumb. He was eager for a fight, and the men simply stared at him when he tried to give them a pep talk.

Charlie Bowers and Curley Henson called Jeff off to one side. The burly Henson wore a sad look. "Jeff, that new lieutenant—he's a friend of yours, ain't he?"

"Well, yes, he is. He's a nice fella too."

"He may be a nice fella," Henson growled, "but he's not going to get me killed! Not if I can help it!"

Young Charlie shook his head in disbelief. "He was tryin' to get the colonel to let us charge the Yankees! Can you believe that? Why, we wouldn't get ten feet before they blew us all to pieces!"

Jeff sighed. "You'll just have to remember it's all new to Cecil. He'll learn quick enough."

"If he doesn't get killed first," Henson groused.

The following afternoon, when Colonel Majors called his officers together for an announcement, Jeff managed to keep within hearing distance. He heard his father say, "Gentlemen, there's going to be an offensive."

"You mean we're going to strike the enemy?" Cecil cried. "Wonderful!"

The other officers, discouraged and weary, stared at the newest officer in the Stonewall Brigade. One of them, standing near Jeff, muttered under his breath, "What are we going to attack them with? Broomsticks?"

If the colonel heard this remark, he ignored it. "General Gordon will lead the attack. We're going to advance, clean the pickets out, and when the obstructions are cleared, we're going to sweep into the fort."

Jeff hurried back to where Tom leaned against the remains of a tree that had mostly been blasted to splinters by Union fire. "Tom, we're going to attack! We're going to attack Fort Stedman!"

Tom straightened up and looked about him. "Then we'd better get the men ready. Make sure they've got enough ammunition. We're about out of powder too."

Jeff stared out over the trenches. "What good will it do to attack, Tom? Even if we took the fort, they'd just take it back. There's so many of them . . ."

Tom didn't try to answer. He limped away, and Jeff rejoined the squad, where he encountered little enthusiasm.

"I don't see how attacking's going to do any good," Henson complained when he heard the plan.

Sgt. Henry Mapes, who had survived the war miraculously all the way from Bull Run, grunted.

"It's not your business to make them decisions, Henson. Just be sure you got plenty of powder."

Jed Hawkins, a small, lean man with black hair, had also been in the army since the beginning. Looking about him, he said, "Every time we attack, or the Yankees attack us, I always think that some of you boys might not be here afterward."

"What about you, Jed?" Jeff asked. "Ever think that *you* might not make it?"

But Jed only laughed. "I got a charmed life. No Yankee slug's ever been made that can get me."

The Southern attack began well enough. The Federal pickets were silenced, the obstructions cleared—but then things began to go wrong. The three other forts that the men were supposed to capture could not be found, and the Confederates' search for them gave the Federals time to recover.

Jeff and his squad found themselves meeting the first wave of the Yankee counterattack. A musket ball cut a twig off a tree by his head, making a peculiar whining sound.

"Come on, let's get out of here," Lieutenant Holey cried. "Retreat! Back to the trenches!"

Jeff was willing enough to go. But as he turned to obey, he saw down the line that Cecil was not retreating. He was going straight forward, despite the commands of his officers to retreat.

"You fool!" Jeff shouted. He expected that he would have no influence on a lieutenant, but he had to try. And then, as he watched, Cecil staggered backward and clutched at his arm.

"Cecil!" Jeff cried, forgetting to use the lieutenant's title. He ran across the field, dimly aware that the bluecoats were advancing. Kneeling, he said, "Are you all right, Cecil?"

Cecil's eyes were glazed with pain. "Jeff—I been shot!"

"Get up, you two!" somebody shouted. "We got to get out of here! Here, let us give you a hand."

Jeff looked up to see other members of his squad. Together, they practically carried Cecil off the field. Some stayed behind to fire final defiant shots at the blue-clad soldiers moving toward them.

When they got the wounded soldier behind the lines, the surgeon took one look at his arm and said, "It'll be back to the hospital for you, Lieutenant."

Cecil had been drugged by the surgeon to kill the pain as the bullet was removed, but by now he had presence of mind enough to reach up and grab Jeff's arm, saying, "Jeff, will you take me back?"

Jeff looked at the boy's pale face and said, "If Pa will let me go, I will."

Colonel Majors, when he heard of Cecil's request, said, "Take a wagon, Jeff. See that he gets to the hospital at Chimborazo. Go by and visit the family on your way back. Tell them we're still holding on."

As Jeff's horse and wagon pulled out of Petersburg, he heard the rumble of the guns behind him and the sharp crackling of musket fire. And all he could think was, *I wish it was all over.*

Looking back at Cecil, he saw that the young man was unconscious. "At least you didn't get killed," he murmured. "If those doctors can save your arm, you'll be better off than the rest of us, because those Yankees are not going to quit!"

4
Flight of an Army

The months in the trenches at Petersburg had drained Jeff of strength. He woke each morning hungry and faint, and others around him were even worse. Each day men limped out of camp or were carried on stretchers behind the lines.

"We can't go on like this, Tom." Jeff had eaten a small portion of cornbread soaked with bacon fat, his portion of the breakfast, and now he looked mournfully at the empty tin plate. "I could eat a horse!"

Tom had finished his own breakfast and lifted his eyes to his brother. "That may be the next thing we'll have to eat." He strained his eyes to see across the trenches through the early morning fog. "They're over there," he murmured, "and I expect we can look for them to come just about any time."

"You think we'll make any more attacks like we did on Fort Stedman?"

"No! The only thing we can do now is run."

"Run?" Jeff stared at his brother doubtfully. "Most of us can't even *walk*, much less run." He glanced toward the rear, where General Lee's headquarters was located. "What do you think General Lee's thinking about this time, Tom? He's got all this on his shoulders."

"He's pulled us out many a time from impossible situations, but I don't think he can do it this time."

Gen. Robert E. Lee had indeed performed military miracles throughout the long years of the Civil War, but now there was nothing more to be done. Richmond would have to be abandoned. Even as Jeff and Tom sat in the mud wondering, Lee was trying to find a way to move his 57,000 remaining men out of the trenches. It was hoped he would meet up with General Johnston and continue the fight elsewhere. He knew that he had only one escape route and that, if he waited too long, Grant would be all over him.

Gen. Philip H. Sheridan, rushing toward Richmond from the Shenandoah Valley with 5,700 cavalrymen, became the key to the Northern strategy. He would later write in his memoirs, "Feeling that the war was nearing its end, I desired my cavalry to be in at its death."

General Lee, on March 29, learned that the Federals were closing in. He sent two officers to make a way for the retreat—Gen. George E. Pickett and his own nephew, Fitzhugh Lee. Ordinarily these were fine officers, but at a spot called Five Forks both Pickett and Fitzhugh Lee made a sad mistake. It was spring, and the shad were running in a nearby river. The two commanding officers were invited to a fish bake, and the two men, as hungry as the rest of the soldiers in the tattered army, eagerly accepted.

Neither Pickett nor Fitzhugh Lee expected to be attacked. However, they were sadly surprised. Sheridan did attack, rushing into the battle, yelling and waving his sword, driving the Federals forward like mad men. The Confederates were defeated.

After the defeat at Five Forks, Jeff and his fellow soldiers were on the march, and no march in the history of the Army of Northern Virginia had been as sad as this one. As they trudged along, Jeff turned to look at his father, coming up from where he had been encouraging the men at the rear. Jeff had not expected his father to stop to talk—he seldom did on a march—so he was surprised when the colonel's worn horse pulled up beside him.

"Are you all right, Corporal?"

"Yes, sir." Jeff looked around at the squad that he had spent so many years with. "We're ready for whatever comes, Colonel."

A thin smile touched Nelson Majors's lips. Long ago he had said that the South would lose, and now he was seeing the curtain come down for the final time. "Don't risk yourself, Jeff. It's over. Stay out of trouble."

"Yes, sir," Jeff said, "and I wish you'd do the same." He plodded along a few more feet and said, "Where we going, Colonel?"

"We're heading for Amelia Courthouse. We're supposed to have wagon trains of food there." He looked down the lines of ill-clad, weary soldiers. "If that food's not there, I don't think we can go on."

April 4 dawned. The Army of Northern Virginia pressed on—30,000 hungry men. Their pace quickened somewhat as they heard the sound of firing off to the south.

"That means Sheridan," Colonel Majors said aloud.

"We better have some food, Colonel," a lieutenant said wearily. "The men can't go much farther."

Jeff was among those who reached Amelia Courthouse at about 8:30, and what they found there was heartbreaking. Despite an abundance of ammunition, not a single ration awaited the famished troops. Hour after hour, starving regiments marched into Amelia Courthouse only to find nothing to eat. Many men at this point simply gave up and melted away into the woods. General Lee rode past his hungry men, and Jeff's squad raised a cheer as he went by.

The night passed, and light showers and wind whipped through the troops as they tried to sleep. All the next day a constant drizzle fell. General Lee wore his gold spurs and his best clothes, but his face was pale, and he knew that the end was near. If his men were well fed and rested, they could outmarch the Federals and join Johnston, but such was not to be.

Finally, on the south side of a small branch of water called Little Sayler's Creek, the two armies met in battle for the final time. It was the last effort of the army of the Confederacy. They had only 7,000 men left to face Sheridan, and it was a hopeless situation. The Federal assault cut into the gray-clad troops, and as the Yankees closed to within yards, a strange silence fell over many in the lines.

Jeff and his friends were not in on that action, but he heard the sound of the guns. Looking around, he said to his brother, "We're surrounded, Tom."

"I reckon so. It's all over."

Somehow, Tom's words brought wild relief to Jeff. He had fought long and hard for the Confederacy. He had buried many good friends. But like his father and Tom himself, he knew that all hope was gone. "I reckon it is, Tom."

On April 7, 1865, General Grant wrote a letter to Gen. Robert E. Lee. It said briefly,

General Robert E. Lee,
Commanding C.S. Army:
General: The results of the last week must convince you of the hopelessness of further resistance on the part of the Army of Northern Virginia in this struggle. I feel that it is so, and regard it as my duty to shift from myself the responsibility of any further effusion of blood by asking you to surrender that portion of the C.S. Army known as the Army of Northern Virginia.
Very respectfully,
your obedient servant

U. S. Grant,
Lieutenant General,
Commanding Armies
of the United States

Lee received the letter, and he, too, wished to stop the bloodshed. As the Confederates marched on past dawn into the bright, warm sunshine of April 8, he thought about that letter. He answered it, asking what terms Grant would make. And then he learned that General Sheridan stood between his forces and the South's last route of escape. It was at a place called Appomattox.

On April 9, General Lee said, "There's nothing left for me to do but go and see General Grant, and I would rather die a thousand deaths!"

The two generals met in the home of a man called Wilmer McLean. McLean had been living near Manasses in Virginia when his life was interrupted by the first battle of the war. He had moved to Appomattox to escape the fighting.

Grant arrived at the McLean house with a terrible headache. He had slept little, his uniform was unpressed, and he looked more like a private soldier than the general of the largest army in the world. General Lee wore his finest uniform.

The two generals met in the living room of the farmhouse and worked out the terms of surrender. Actually, there were no hard terms laid down. At one point Lee said, "The men in our army own their own horses. Would it be permitted for them to take them home?"

General Grant assured Lee he would see to it that the men kept their horses. He would also give orders that the Southern soldiers be allowed free passage on all government transportation in order to reach their homes.

The two generals parted, and for all practical purposes the Civil War was over.

5
Jeff Stacks His Musket

Three soldiers wearing blue uniforms moved forward as a part of Grant's vast army. All three had fought in Tennessee but had been shifted to the last battles in Virginia. One of them, Royal Carter, wore the stripes of a sergeant. The two who marched beside him were privates.

Drake Bedford glanced at his close friend Pvt. A. B. Rose. "Well, Rosie, I guess we're about going to wind it up today."

Rosie, a tall, gangling soldier with huge feet and tow-colored hair, put his light blue eyes on Drake Bedford. "Sure wish I had some of my liver medicine with me," he moaned. "I figure I'm going to need it."

Bedford, tall and darkly handsome, laughed aloud. "You never had a sick day in your life! You're just a hypochondriac."

Rosie stared at his friend sadly. "You just don't understand what a sick man I am, and I lost all my medicine in Tennessee."

"Yes, but you got a fiancée instead!" Royal said. He nudged Drake with his elbow. "Can you imagine old Rosie here a married man?"

"As well as I can imagine you, Sergeant," Drake said. "You're just as engaged as he is."

Quickly Royal glanced up at the tall private. He had to look up, for Royal was not tall, though thick and strong. He was often called "The Professor" by the soldiers, for he had spent some time in college. He thought of the rivalry between himself and Drake Bedford over Lorraine Jenkins. He thought, *Drake's taking it well, losing Lori. I don't believe I could have done as well if I had lost her to him.* Aloud he said, "I don't reckon we'll get married until we get back in Kentucky."

Drake grinned, showing no ill feelings. He had been recently converted, and the change in him had been almost unbelievable. "Well, you fellas are all taken up, but I'm gonna relish gettin' back and bein' a returning hero. Every girl in Pineville will be wantin' to get her hands on me."

The three soldiers were not at all unhappy that the war was over. They had fought in some of the final battles, and it had been Royal's constant fear that in some battle he might encounter the Confederate soldier who had been his best friend for years, Tom Majors. Fortunately, Royal's unit had engaged in little actual fighting, and now, on April 12, he was glad that the order had come to review the stacking of muskets by the Confederate army.

"It seems strange, not fightin'," Rosie murmured. They were tramping down the Richmond-Lynchburg Road, which led from the Confederate camps across the north branch of the Appomattox to a slope beyond the courthouse.

"Sure is," Drake agreed, "and for my part, I'm glad it's over."

"I think we're all glad it's over," Royal said.

Then a command came, and their lieutenant came to a halt, saying, "Look, there's the Confederates."

Eagerly Royal searched the ranks of ragged soldiers that had formed on the square. He was looking for any one of the Majorses, and soon he whispered, "There he is! There he is! There's Colonel Majors."

There was no sign of General Lee, but another general had dismounted and was now standing in front of the Confederate ranks.

Royal continued to search the Southern lines, and then he saw Tom Majors—behind his father and flanked by Jeff. "There they are!" he said. "All three of them. Thank God they've all made it through the war!"

"That's right unusual," Drake said, "for a family to get through without losing somebody." He looked over the surrendered troops and said sadly, "They don't look too good, do they?"

"No, they don't," Royal agreed.

The Confederates, without drum or fife, marched forward in the measured tread that had become part of their souls.

"They sure been whittled down," Drake said quietly.

"So have we." Royal looked around at the Union's remnants of units from Massachusetts, Maine, Michigan, Maryland, Pennsylvania, and New York. He thought of all the men who lay in graves scattered across the South.

Then he turned to watch as the Southerners came with their swinging route step and swaying battle flags. In front was the proud Confederate insignia, the great field of white with a canton of star-strewn cross of blue on a field of red.

Royal watched as General Gordon and his men approached. He saw the Union general, Joshua Chamberlain, speak to an aide, who called the Federals to stiff attention.

"Carry arms!"

Gordon rode by at the head of his column of men. Few eyes were dry on either side as the ragged yet proud Confederates passed, made their salutes, then dropped their rifles, bayonets, cartridge boxes, and flags in heaps beyond a triangle just east of the courthouse.

As the men filed by, Royal suddenly found himself looking into the face of Tom Majors. Tom missed a step, so that the man behind bumped into him, and the two men who had been friends since their boyhood days stared at each other in profound silence.

Glancing to his right, Jeff saw his brother and the Union soldier caught up in the moment.

And then he reached the stack of muskets. Though some threw down their weapons with anger, Jeff laid his down tenderly. He knew he was saying good-bye to part of his life, a part that he would never forget, and he felt, once again, tears sting his eyes.

Jeff marched on with the rest of the Confederates, and finally 26,000 men were paroled. But no one now thought of numbers or victory.

General Chamberlain wrote later of the ceremony, "On our part not a sound of a trumpet more, no roll of drum; not a cheer, not word nor whisper of vain-glorying, nor emotion of man standing again at the order, but an odd stillness rather, and breath holding, as if it were the passing of the dead."

And then it was done. Jeff marched away beside his brother, his eye on his father up ahead. He was thinking that those who had followed Lee for so long must now travel their own separate roads. He wondered what kind of life would be left for him and for his family, and what they would make of the new.

Tom, still marching alongside Jeff, limping slightly from the inconvenience of his artificial leg, asked, "Did you see Royal?"

"Sure. He was looking right at us. It was funny, sort of. You two have been friends all your life. Now you're wearing gray, and he's wearing blue."

Tom Majors looked down at his tattered uniform and shook his head. "Neither one of us will be wearing a uniform much longer. We'll have to find something else to wear."

But Tom's thoughts were on Sarah, Royal Carter's sister, whom he had loved for years. Now he was not only a man with just one leg—he was an ex-Rebel besides. Sadness came over him as he thought, *There's too much against all of us. We can't ever be what we would've been if it hadn't been for the war.*

6
Where Can We Go?

Before the Confederate army left Richmond, abandoning it to the Federals, they set fire to the city's warehouses, and the fire quickly spread. Soon the streets were filled with a mob of thugs, thieves, prostitutes, army deserters, and convicts who had broken out of the penitentiary. All order broke down. To make matters worse, the city's liquor supply had been emptied into the gutters, where rough-looking people immediately began scooping up the whiskey in buckets and pitchers.

Then Lee's army streamed northward across the Appomattox, and as the last Confederate defender of Richmond galloped over the bridge, everyone then understood that the war was truly over.

Soon Federal troops filled the streets of Richmond. One fourteen-year-old girl, Francis Hunt, reflected in her diary, "The Yankees are behaving very well considering it is them."

Abraham Lincoln decided to visit Richmond. Accompanied by his twelve-year-old son, he arrived unannounced. But as he was recognized, some black laborers fell to their knees and kissed his feet—which Lincoln helplessly protested. Then they came tumbling and shouting about him, and the president stood a chance of being crushed.

Lincoln said only a few words. "You're free," he told them, "as free as air."

One of the most touching moments in Lincoln's life came when he paid a visit to Mrs. George Pickett, the pretty young wife of the Confederate general. Answering the door, Mrs. Pickett found a tall, gaunt, sad-faced man in ill-fitting clothes standing outside.

He said, "I'm Abraham Lincoln."

When she gasped, "The president!" he said, "No, Abraham Lincoln, ma'am. Just George's old friend."

Lincoln took the Picketts' ten-month-old son, kissed him, then handed the child back, saying, "Tell your father that I forgive him for the sake of your bright eyes."

"Well, the house is still there," Colonel Majors said, heaving a sigh of relief. "I was afraid it might have been burned by some of the rabble."

Jeff and Tom and their father had walked all the way back from Appomattox to Richmond, for no ride had presented itself. When Tom protested that it was a shame for an officer to have to walk, his father said, "I'm not an officer anymore. We're all paroled out. Remember, there *is* no more Confederacy."

Now, as they anxiously approached the familiar white frame house, Nelson cried, "Hello! We're back!"

Instantly the door burst open, and Eileen came running out, her red hair unbound and catching the April breeze. She threw herself into his arms and pressed her face against his chest. She was sobbing. "You're back! You're back! I was so afraid!"

He patted her shoulders and held her tightly. "It's all right, Eileen," he whispered. "We're all right now. The war is over."

Jeff got an equally ardent welcome, for Leah ran out of the house next. She threw herself at Jeff, knocking him off balance. He had to hold onto her to keep from falling down. She was sobbing too.

"Now," he muttered, "there's no sense to make such a fuss."

Leah looked up at him, tears running down her face. "We were so afraid. We heard rumors that the whole army had been killed."

"Why, that's foolish!" Jeff said. He felt strange holding Leah in his arms like this. She was not a little girl any longer but a grown young lady. He hardly knew how to speak to her. "Well, I'm all right," he said finally.

Tom was grinning. "You don't have to hold her any longer." He had picked up Esther, who was squealing and holding onto his neck and pulling at his cap. "He tried to get himself shot so you'd feel sorry for him and make a hero out of him," Tom teased. "But he couldn't get in the way of a bullet."

"Don't make fun, Tom!" Leah said quickly. Her lip was quivering, and she stepped back with her cheeks reddened. She was visibly embarrassed now by the way she had greeted Jeff.

Eileen pulled herself free from her husband, saying, "Come inside the house. We want to hear everything that's happened. There's not much left to eat, I'm afraid, but we can scrape up something."

The women found five eggs, bits and pieces of bacon, two loaves of bread that Leah had baked the day before, and a jar of blackberry jam.

"Why, this is a feast," Nelson said, after he had asked the blessing over the simple meal. "We haven't had a meal this good since . . . well, I don't know when."

"Tastes good, doesn't it, Pa? I don't reckon I have to call you 'Colonel' anymore, do I?" Jeff asked.

"No, not anymore!" His father reached for a slice of bread. "I thank God that we're all safe."

Tom was nibbling at a piece of bacon. "Not many families got through without losing a single man. God's been extra good to us."

Quiet fell, and Jeff could sense happiness all about the table at that moment.

After the meal, Tom took Esther outside to play, and Jeff, seeing his father looking at his new wife, whispered to Leah, "Let's go down to the pond."

"All right, Jeff."

They sat on a log by the water.

"I didn't mean to grab you like that, Jeff," Leah apologized. She flushed. "I guess I just got carried away."

"Aw, that's all right. I'm glad to be welcomed home. Do it any time you want to."

Leah's eyes flashed at his teasing. She pushed at him.

"Look out! You're going to push me off the log!"

The pond was still, but suddenly, near their feet, an enormous bullfrog croaked something that sounded like, "Yikes!" and with a mighty splash broke the quietness of the water.

Jeff looked at the rings spreading out over the pond. "I'll come back and get you," he promised the frog. "I haven't had any good frog legs in quite a while."

"Let's go frogging tonight. We could use something different to eat," Leah said.

"All right. The boat's still here, if we can get a frog gig."

"We have the same one we used last time." Leah moved closer to him. "Tell me about what it was like at the surrender."

Jeff stirred slightly, not wanting to talk about it, but he saw that she really wanted to hear. He recounted how the Southern troops had all lined up, and the Northern troops had presented arms to them.

"And guess who I saw as I was going to stack my musket."

"Who? General Grant?"

"No, it was Royal."

"*Royal?* My brother?"

"He's the only Royal I know. Yep, he was looking right at us, and he had Rosie and Drake Bedford right beside him. All three of them made it through."

"Oh, how wonderful! I wonder if he'll come to see us."

"He will if he gets a chance. You know that."

It was barely ten o'clock in the morning when Royal Carter knocked at the door of the white frame house. From inside, he heard Leah say, "I'll go see who it is."

She opened the door, cried, "Royal!" and threw her arms around his neck.

Royal laughed and held her close. "Hello, sis," he said. "I brought some company."

Leah untwined her arms and greeted Rosie and Drake.

Tom and Jeff rose at once and came over to shake hands. The boys had all known each other before the war.

"It's good to see you, Royal—and all of you," Tom said. "I saw you at the surrender."

Royal could not speak for a moment. He had always admired Tom Majors more than any other man he knew. A lump came into his throat as he said, "I'm glad you're all right, Tom. I worried about you."

"I worried about you too."

"Well, everybody stop worrying." Rosie grinned. "The war is over."

Nelson Majors greeted the three Union soldiers he had known back in Kentucky. He introduced Eileen. Then everybody sat down, and Leah made sassafras tea and served the remnants of some cookies she had baked for Jeff and Tom the night before.

After they had talked a while, Nelson said, "I guess you fellas will be going back to Kentucky."

"As soon as we can get there. We'll be mustered out pretty quick, I imagine," Royal said. "What about you, sir?"

"We haven't made up our mind yet. I don't see what we're going to do. There's not going to be any work anywhere with two million men suddenly turned loose out of the armies."

Royal looked up quickly. He studied the face of the older Majors and then saw the same concern on the faces of his sons. "I don't think there's any problem about that, Colonel."

"Not 'Colonel' anymore, Royal." But then he asked curiously, "And what do you mean? There *is* a problem. There are lots of men just like me with nothing to go back to."

Royal had been considering for some time the plight of those who had left the North and the border states to fight for the Confederacy. Especially he had thought of the Majorses. He glanced again at his friend Tom, who looked especially downcast.

"Why, you're going back to Kentucky. There's nothing else for you to do."

Nelson looked up with surprise. "We can't do that."

"Can't do it? Why not?"

"For one thing, there's nothing there for us. We sold our place there, and now the money's all gone."

Royal shook his head emphatically. "I'm surprised at you, sir. You've got friends back in Kentucky."

"I've got enemies too," Nelson said abruptly. "Not everyone will want to see an ex-Rebel come back to Pineville."

"I reckon that might be true," Rosie spoke up, "but there's lots of us that would. And I guess those of us that want you can convince those that don't that they're wrong."

Tom said, "Thank you, Rosie. That's a kind heart speaking."

"But what Rosie says is true," Drake broke in. "You spent all your life in Pineville before the war. Now it's over. It's time to put it behind us. I think you ought to go back."

Royal saw Leah look eagerly at Jeff, and then everyone studied the face of Nelson Majors.

Eileen said, "It might be best, Nelson."

But he still seemed unconvinced. "We'll just have to think about it, Royal—but I appreciate what you've said."

After the three Federal soldiers left, Leah said, "Royal is right, sir. My family would all be glad to see you come back."

"I'd be coming back a beggar," he said. "We don't even have the money to *get* to Kentucky."

"Well, God's got the money," Jeff said. "Let's do it, Pa! There's nothing here for us in Virginia. Just bad memories about this war. Let's go back to the hills where we came from."

Jeff's father stared at him, then shifted his gaze to his older son. "What do you think, Tom?"

"I agree with Jeff. There's nothing for us here."

Silence fell over the room as everyone watched the face of the tall, dark-haired man wearing the ragged uniform of a Confederate colonel.

Finally he took a deep breath, expelled it, then nodded. "All right, we'll go to Kentucky."

Jeff cried, "Hooray!" He picked up Esther and tossed her into the air. "You're going to Kentucky, Esther!"

"Kentucky!" Esther cried and squealed as Jeff tossed her again.

Eileen laid a hand on Nelson's shoulder. "We'll be all right," she said. "I'd rather our child would be born away from here."

"We won't have much. I don't know how we'll make it."

"God will make a way."

"When can we go, Pa?" Jeff said.

Now that the decision was made, it appeared Nelson Majors burned to get away from all the bad memories of Petersburg and Richmond. "I guess we're ready for sunup in the morning."

Leah squeezed Jeff's hand. "We'll all go together, Jeff. It'll be just like it used to be," she whispered.

"I don't think it could ever be that," he whispered back. He smiled at this glorious young woman who had grown up in the few years since they had left Kentucky. "But I'll be glad to get back home."

7

Home

The departure from Richmond did not take place as easily as Nelson Majors had hoped. Although General Grant had assured soldiers rides on public transportation, the trains overflowed with men trying to get home. Many set forth walking, but Nelson knew that this would not do for his family. Eileen had to have something better than a walk back to Kentucky.

For two days he worried about how to get a wagon, horses, some means of transportation. He said little to the family, but he was gone most of those two days trying to arrange something. When he came back home at the end of the second day, however, he was greeted by an old friend, Uncle Silas, Leah's elderly uncle.

"Silas! You're back!"

"I surely am, boy, and just in time to do a job, it seems."

Silas had a fine white beard and bright blue eyes. He had had the good fortune to put his money into Northern stocks before the war, so that now the fall of the Confederacy had not bankrupted him.

"I guess they've been telling you we're going back to Kentucky, Silas," Nelson said when they were seated at the kitchen table.

"That they have, and I'm of a mind to make the trip with you. I haven't seen my family there in quite a while."

"Well, you may get there before we do!"

"How do you figure that?"

Nelson shrugged wearily. "I can't find any way to get back there. I don't have any money, and if I did, I'm not sure I could buy a decent carriage or wagon."

Silas laughed, brushing his mustache back. "I wish we'd never have problems any worse than that! I've just come in from Charlotte," he said. "Didn't you see that new buckboard outside there?"

"Yes, I did . . ."

"Well, it's a fine one, and a fine team too. Out at my place in the country there's a good wagon I brought back too, with another good team. Enough to haul this furniture, and all of us all the way to Kentucky."

"You see! Didn't I tell you, Pa?" Jeff said. "I knew God would look out for us."

Leah suddenly reached over and kissed her uncle on the cheek. "You're an angel, Uncle Silas."

Silas muttered with some embarrassment, "Well, now, nobody ever actually called me an angel before. Not that I mind it, of course." His eyes twinkled as he looked back at Nelson Majors. "So we got a wagon, and a nice carriage for you and your missus and Leah here. We can figure out what to take with us out of this house to set up housekeeping back in Kentucky."

Nelson stared at the old man. "We won't have a house to put it in, I'm afraid."

"If God can provide furniture, Pa," Tom said eagerly, "He can provide a house." He leaned over and slapped Silas on the shoulder with such force that the old man wheezed. "Thank you, Uncle Silas. You've always come through."

56

The next day, Royal showed up. He had somehow wangled a wagon and a team from the Federal army, which had plenty. "I knew you'd be needing some transportation," he said. "This'll help. We can all go back together."

There was hurrying, and working together, and loading with almost desperate speed. And on the next day the little caravan pulled out from war-torn Richmond.

With Eileen by his side, Nelson drove the carriage. In the backseat sat Uncle Silas and Leah and Esther. Silas had even sold his property, saying, "I'll never come back to Virginia again. I want to be with my family." And behind the carriage came two wagons packed full of household goods. Royal drove the first wagon, with Jeff and Tom on the seat beside him. Rosie and Drake followed them with the other team.

As the little procession left Richmond, Jeff turned and looked back on the city, which was sad, indeed, to behold. "Not much left of it, is there?" he murmured.

"No, but it will be rebuilt," Royal said. "The whole South will have to rebuild."

"I guess so," Jeff muttered. The sight of the city depressed him. Still, he agreed with Royal. "Things look pretty bad, but they'll make it."

"Sure they will," Tom said cheerfully and clapped him on the back. "So will we. Now then, let's get on with it."

Royal slapped the backs of the horses with the lines. "We'll be all right," he said, "as soon as we get home."

The campfire crackled pleasantly, and its yellow

flame was a warming dot in the darkness beside the creek. The smell of frying bacon was in the air as Leah and Eileen cooked supper.

Jeff and Tom were at the small stream that formed an elbow around the campsite. The two were gathering more dried wood. It was not cold, but a fire made a cheerful sight in the gloom that gathered under the tall oak trees.

"I'm glad to be going home, Tom."

Tom did not answer for a moment, and Jeff was surprised. "*You're* glad, aren't you?"

"Well, of course, I am, but things are pretty much confused."

Jeff knew his brother well. "You're thinking about Sarah, aren't you?"

Tom looked at him. A half-moon was overhead, throwing down silver beams, illuminating his face. "Can't hide anything from you, can I? Yes, I've been thinking about Sarah."

"She loves you, Tom."

"She loves what I used to be."

The reply was gloomy, and Jeff knew Tom was thinking about his missing leg. "You're not worrying about that again? You don't have to worry."

"I still do. Sarah could marry anybody. A beautiful girl like her. Why should she want half a man?"

"You're not half a man!" Jeff said shortly. "You're the same as you always were. Why, you can ride, and walk, and work. That artificial leg, it's almost as good as a real leg."

"'Almost' isn't the same thing. I'm not what I used to be. I'll always be a step behind other fellows."

"Tom, you've got to stop thinking like this." Jeff picked up another piece of dead wood. "God's been so good to bring us all through. You could've been dead, or Pa, or me!"

Tom suddenly laughed. "You're right, Jeff. Of course, you're right. But a fellow can't help thinking about it. Come on, let's go back to the fire."

They were at the top of a high hill, and the horses were tired from the climb.

"Well, there it is," Nelson said to Eileen, gesturing down at the placid valley that lay between two sections of rising, rolling hills.

"Oh, it's beautiful, Nelson!"

He looked out over the valley for a while, then said, "It's home—at least it used to be."

Eileen held onto his arm. "It will be again. You'll see." She knew that he was worried about their reception back in Pineville and tried to cheer him up as the carriage and wagons started downhill. "We'll get a place, and then the baby will come, and Tom will marry Sarah."

"And I suppose someday Jeff and Leah will get married." Nelson nodded.

"I bet they do."

"They'll have to wait a while. It's going to be hard for boys like Tom and Jeff and the others, starting from nothing. We don't even have a farm to work."

"God will take care of us."

"You always believe that, don't you?"

"So do you," Eileen said. "You're just grumpy. Come on now, let's think of names for the baby."

Nelson turned to her. "I've got a good one."

"What is it?"

"Hezekiah. We could call him Hezzie."

"What if it's a girl?" Eileen's dimples suddenly appeared. "Would you want to call her Hezzie?"

"It'd be better than Hydrangea, wouldn't it?"

Eileen was happy. She had succeeded in taking Nelson's mind off his worries.

As they moved along the twisting road that led down the mountain, he pointed out spots that he had known. Cabins where old friends lived. And then he said, "There it is. There's the Carter place. I bet Leah and Royal are about to jump out and run."

When the caravan got closer to the Carter house, Leah did suddenly jump out of the carriage, crying, "Ma! Pa! We're home!"

The door opened, and three people burst out of the house.

Dan Carter led the way. He caught up Leah in his arms, exclaiming, "Well, now, daughter. You're back again! Back home!"

"Yes, I am, Pa!" Leah cried, kissing him. She embraced her mother, then her sister Sarah. "We're all here—Royal and Jeff and Tom and their father and the new Mrs. Majors and Rosie and Drake . . ."

By now Royal had leaped out of the second wagon and was running forward to greet his folks. He hugged them all and then looked around eagerly. "Where's Lori—and Charlie?"—the two girls who had fled the war in Tennessee to wait in Pineville.

"Those brides-to-be have gone to town. If they'd only known you were coming . . ." Mrs. Carter said. She hugged her son again. "You're looking fine, and you've picked a fine wife. We all love Lori."

As soon as Nelson had introduced Eileen, Rosie came forward, his eyes gleaming. "You haven't seen a young heifer around here named Charlie, have you?"

"Rosie, you ought to be ashamed of yourself!" Sarah exclaimed. "You don't speak of your fiancée like that!"

"Well, I don't know if I'll live long enough to get married. It seems like I been havin' lots of ailments lately."

No one wanted to hear about Rosie's imaginary ailments.

And now Sarah was turning to face Tom, who got slowly down from the wagon and approached her.

Leah expected Tom to take Sarah in his arms, but he simply pulled his hat off and stood there, saying, "Hello, Sarah."

If Sarah was disappointed at the sparseness of his greeting, she tried not to show it. "Hello, Tom," she said. She hesitated and put out her hand.

He took it, then stepped back. "I guess I'd better get these horses unhitched. They're pretty tired."

Sarah turned away, tears in her eyes, and Leah whispered, "He'll be all right, Sarah. You'll see."

At that moment Ezra Payne appeared. He let out a whoop, for he had been good friends with Leah and Jeff. After he shook hands with everybody and nearly everyone had started toward the house, Ezra turned to Leah. "I don't guess you heard about me, did you?"

"Heard what, Ezra?"

"I'm courtin' Helen McGee down the road a piece."

"Why, I think that's wonderful, Ezra! She's a fine girl. Are you going to get married?"

"If she'll ever have me, I will. I guess there's going to be a lot of marrying going on. Rosie marrying up with Miss Charlene, and Royal marrying

61

Lori Jenkins. And then, of course, there's Miss Sarah and Dewitt Falor."

Tom was unhitching the horses, and he turned and looked at Ezra. "What's this about Dewitt Falor?"

"You don't know about him?" Ezra asked innocently. "He's been courtin' her for up to a year now. His pa's the richest man in the valley, you know. I reckon he'd be quite a catch for Sarah."

Tom stared at the tall, young hired man and said through stiff lips. "I guess it would be." He limped away, leading the horses off toward the barn.

Instantly Leah turned to Ezra. "I wish you hadn't said that!"

He was astonished. "But everybody knows it. Dewitt's been talkin' for a long time now about how he intends to marry Sarah."

"What does Sarah say?"

Ezra shrugged. "She doesn't talk about it, but, of course, most people around here know that Dewitt Falor gets pretty much anything he wants."

"I'll bet he won't get Sarah," Leah said with an angry light in her eyes as Ezra headed toward the barn.

She went over to Jeff. "Did you hear what Ezra said?"

"I sure did. I didn't like it. Tom feels bad as it is."

"It won't come to anything. Sarah doesn't love anybody but Tom."

Jeff, however, seemed not so sure. "I don't know, Leah. A lot's happened since we left. Sarah may have changed her mind."

"I don't believe it!"

Inside the house, she quickly found a time to whisper to Sarah, "What's Ezra talking about—you and Dewitt Falor?"

Sarah's cheeks flushed. "I wish he hadn't said that. I haven't done a thing to encourage Dewitt."

"He thinks he's going to marry you."

"I know he does, but he's wrong."

"Why don't you just tell him so?"

"I have told him so, and I'll tell him again," Sarah said. "But you know Dewitt. He's bullheaded, and he's always gotten everything he wanted. Now he's got his mind set on me."

"How about Tom?" Leah asked abruptly.

Sarah turned and looked at her younger sister. Quietly she said, "I've always loved Tom. Ever since we were sixteen years old. I still do—and I always will."

Leah threw her arms around Sarah, whispering, "Oh, I'm so glad!" Then she drew back and frowned. "But Tom feels bad about not having any money. And he's back to worrying about losing his leg."

"I know, and he won't let me show how I feel about him."

"We'll find a way," Leah said.

Sarah smiled. "You're quite a little matchmaker, aren't you?"

"Well, somebody has to do it!"

Supper was a feast. The crops had been good, and Ezra slaughtered a yearling so that they could have a barbecue. The delicious smell of roasting meat filled the Carters' yard, and a festive air was about the place.

When they all were gathered around the dining room table, Dan Carter asked a long and earnest—and excited—blessing over the food. He ended by saying, "And God, we're glad that our friends and neighbors are back home again. In the name of Jesus we thank You. Amen."

Every place at the table was filled, and extra chairs had been brought in. The table seemed to groan under the weight of the meat and vegetables and glasses of tea and cider.

There was happy laughter—and talk, not the least of which was between Rosie and his fiancée, Charlie Satterfield. She was a tall girl from the hills of Georgia. She had fallen in love with Drake at first, but it was Rosie who had finally won her heart. She sat beside him, her curly hair framing her face, and she smiled shyly as Drake teased her about becoming a bride.

Across the table, Lori Jenkins sat as close as she could to Royal. These two had had a long courtship. Lori was a small girl with auburn hair, brown eyes, and an oval face. She was very pretty and very much in love.

At the foot of the table sat Nelson with Uncle Silas on his right and Eileen on his left. After the babble had died down somewhat, he said, "Dan, you're looking at a man who doesn't have one single idea in his head about what to do next."

Mr. Carter, who loved the Majorses as if they were his own flesh and blood, said, "Let God make the plans. You just wait until He tells you what they are."

Nelson grinned abruptly and looked at Eileen. "There's our theology. We just wait on God."

Eileen took his hand. "I can't think of a better way to live."

The former colonel looked about the table. "I thank God for bringing us back here, but I don't want to be a burden on anybody."

"God owns the cattle on a thousand hills, and He owns all the hills," Uncle Silas said suddenly. "Don't ever sell God short, Nelson."

"That's right." Dan Carter nodded. "He's going to provide for His own, and you're His own." He looked around the crowded room then. "Don't anybody eat too much. I think I smelled some peach pie cookin' earlier in the day!"

Rosie said dolefully, "That's good. My stomach's been actin' up, and I reckon peach pie's just the thing to calm it down some."

And Leah looked across at Jeff, thinking, *When he was fourteen, I thought he was the handsomest boy I ever saw—and now he's the handsomest man.*

From across the table, Jeff was looking at Leah. He appreciated her green eyes and blonde hair and the smoothness of her skin. *There's gonna be lots of fellas come courting Leah.* He remembered the old days when they had hunted birds' eggs together. *I reckon courting's a little bit different from hunting birds' eggs.*

Studying her more closely as she laughed and her white teeth flashed, he thought, *But she's pretty enough to fight for, and that's what I aim to do!*

8

"Go Home, Rebel!"

Finding a place to live proved to be both complicated and simple.

Although the Carters would have been glad to put up the three Majors men and Mrs. Majors, Nelson was almost frantic with anxiety to be in his own house.

"I appreciate your offer, Dan," he said the morning after they arrived, "but you know how it is. A man just needs his own place."

Dan Carter nodded slowly. "Ordinarily I'd agree with you, Nelson, but situations change. Right now you're in kind of a bind. It looks to me like the best thing for your wife would be to stay here and let us kind of take care of her." He scratched his thinning hair and shook his head. "She doesn't seem too pert, does she?"

"No, she's not well. She had trouble with her first child, and that worries me." Nelson shuffled his feet. The two men were standing in the yard, and Nelson had just saddled a horse. "I'm going to ride around and look. There's bound to be some kind of house I can get around here. It's just that I don't have any money to pay for it. I may have to work it off."

"You can always count on me for a loan."

"No, you've done enough, Dan. Taking care of my daughter during the war—and now welcoming us back. I've got to do something on my own."

He mounted and rode away to spend the better part of the day covering the roads. He was greeted by many with warm smiles—people who had been sympathetic to the Confederacy. Others slammed their doors in his face. After one such encounter, he said to himself, *I knew to expect this, but it's hard from old friends. Still, I can't blame them.*

He returned to the Carter place just at twilight, and as he stepped down from the horse, Eileen came to meet him. "Did you find anything, Nelson?"

"Not a thing, but I'll try again tomorrow."

"Come on in the house. We kept supper warm for you."

"What have you been doing all day?"

"Sewing baby clothes. Mary's such a wonderful seamstress. I'll show you the nightgowns that I made for Hezekiah."

"You're not really going to name a helpless baby Hezekiah?"

"It was your suggestion." She smiled, humor glowing in her eyes. "Unless you can come up with something better, I think it'll be Hezekiah."

"*Anything* would be better."

They went inside. The meal was already over, and only Dan and Uncle Silas still remained at the table. The others had all scattered.

"Hello, Nelson," Silas said cheerfully. "Sit down and get on the outside of some of this good food that Mary and Sarah made up for you."

"I can use it. Hungry work riding the roads."

He sat and listened as Dan and Silas talked about the farm. Neither of them mentioned the war, and he was grateful for that.

Then Mary Carter brought in a plateful of food and gave him a big smile. She was a compassionate woman with the same blonde hair and green eyes as could be seen in her daughter Leah. She fixed herself a cup of tea and sat down as Nelson ate.

"I couldn't find anything—that we could afford," Nelson said, in answer to her question. When the others all looked at him, he grinned wryly. "Of course, I can't afford much of anything."

Mrs. Carter got up to bring him a cup of tea. At his words she paused and said, "I wasn't going to say anything about it, Nelson, but there's always the old Turner place."

"Aren't the Turners still there?"

"Oh, no," she said. "They moved out two years ago. Nobody's lived in the old house since."

"Did Turner sell out?"

"I don't think he sold out," Dan Carter said. "The bank foreclosed on the place. Now, that's an idea, wife. That old place is just sitting vacant. Of course, it's a mess. It wasn't much when the Turners had it, and it's worse now."

"I'll stop in the bank tomorrow and see if they'll let me rent it."

"I should think they would. Anything they get out of it is profit. Nobody wants that old place. It was wore out when Turner bought it, and he finished it off. Only about ten acres, I think, but the house—at least it's a roof."

Nelson sipped the tea that Mary had brought for him. "I'll go in tomorrow morning."

After he and Eileen had gone to bed, they lay talking quietly.

"I hope we get that house, Nelson."

"You may not be after you see it. It always was pretty much a wreck. I'm surprised it's still standing."

"Anything will do."

Nelson took her hand. "I didn't bring you much, Eileen."

She squeezed his hand tightly, and moonlight illuminated her smile. "You brought me yourself, and that's the best gift of all."

Pineville had not changed greatly, Nelson saw as he rode down the main street. It never had been a large town, although it was the county seat. He saw that several new stores had been added during the years he had been gone, but mostly the place looked about the same as when he'd left it. He was greeted several times by old friends—and ignored by others, who gave him one hard look and then turned away.

He drew up in front of the bank, a frame building wedged between a dry goods store and a hardware, and tied the horse to the rail. The assistant manager, a tall, gaunt man named Robert Squires, greeted him with merely a grunt and a nod. Squires had been strongly Union, Nelson remembered, and had been hateful to the Majors family even before he had left for the South.

"Why, hello, Mr. Squires. Is Dave in?"

"Mr. Pimberly is in," Squires said stiffly, "but I don't know if he'll see you."

"Would you mind asking?"

Without another word, Squires sniffed, then stepped through a door at the back of the room. He came out shortly and said reluctantly, "You can go in now."

"Thanks for your courtesy, Squires."

Stepping into the back room, Nelson advanced to the large walnut desk and greeted the man behind it.

"Hello, Dave."

He waited, for he knew that Dave Pimberly had also been a Union man, and he expected that the banker would greet him coldly.

Pimberly, however, got up smiling. He stuck his hand across the desk and gripped Nelson's with a firm pressure. "I'm glad to see you made it through, Nelson. And your boys too, I hear."

"Yes, we did. Thank God for that. How about your family?"

"We lost Mackey at Gettysburg."

"I'm sorry to hear it. He had a great deal of promise, Mackey did."

"Yes, I guess you might say all those that fell had a great deal of promise," Pimberly said. "Sit down, Nelson. Tell me what you've been doing."

Lowering himself into the oak chair across from the banker, Nelson sighed heavily. "I guess you might say I'm not doing anything, Dave. Got mustered out of the army and thought about staying in Virginia." He looked out the window to where a pair of robins perched in a tree, one of them feeding worms to a baby. He studied the sight for a moment, then turned back to Pimberly. "But this is home to me—at least I'd like for it to be."

Pimberly studied him. He had known Nelson most of his life. They had disagreed about politics and about the war, but Pimberly now said quietly, "You're going to find some folks who are not glad to see you—but you expected that."

"Yes, I did. I'll just have to prove myself, I suppose."

"We're going to have to learn to live together, North and South," Pimberly remarked. He leaned forward and asked, "What can I do for you, Nelson?"

"I was talking with Dan Carter about the old Turner place. I need a place to put my family."

"You want to buy it? Not much to it, you know. You remember the place."

"I can't buy it. In the first place, I don't have any money, and if I did, it wouldn't be to buy that. What I want to do is rent the old house."

Pimberly shook his head doubtfully. "It's not fit to live in. You're married now, I understand from Dan."

"Yes, and my wife's going to have a baby."

"Then you don't want that old shack."

"Not much choice, Dave. If you'd rent it to me, we'll fix it up. We'll make do for a while."

"Move in any time you like. It's not worth any rent. Actually, I thought you'd come in to ask for a loan."

"Not yet, Dave. I appreciate your kindness."

Nelson got up, shook the banker's hand, and left the bank.

He had not gone more than ten steps down the street toward the general store when a voice called out, "Go home, Rebel! Go back to the South where you belong!"

Looking up quickly, he saw three men standing across the street. He did not recognize two of them, but one of them he knew at once. Young Dewitt Falor. Falor was glaring at him with anger in his eyes.

Nelson felt a streak of annoyance go through him. He almost stepped into the street to cross and challenge the men. Then he remembered that he had to live with these people and that starting a

71

fight would not be the best way to begin. He went on down to the store and picked up a few groceries.

The clerk, who knew him, said, "Now, you can't pay for those with Confederate money, Nelson."

"I know that, Sy." Nelson reached into his pocket and pulled out some greenbacks that he had been forced to borrow from Silas. "These will spend, won't they?"

Relief washed over Sy's face. "Sure, they're fine. Glad to have you back."

Nelson left the store, mounted the horse, and started home. As he left town, he heard again a voice filled with raw anger call out, "Go back where you belong, Rebel!"

"The breeze feels good, Jeff," Leah said.

"Sure does. It's been a hot day!"

The two had gone for a late-afternoon walk and now were some two miles from the Carter house. Leah had chosen to wear her pale blue dress today, and her hair was tied back with a dark green ribbon. Jeff had on a pair of faded jeans and a worn white shirt. His hair, as black as hair could possibly be, framed the olive skin of his face. She thought he looked very tall and lean and handsome as they walked along together.

Looking up suddenly, he pointed, "You see that hickory tree over there?"

"Sure. What about it?" she asked, puzzled.

"Don't you remember that tree?"

It was an enormous hickory that had limbs stretching out in all directions.

"That's where we found that hairy woodpecker's egg. We'd looked for it for two years. I'm surprised you'd forget."

Leah clapped her hands together and smiled. She ran to the tree and reached up to touch a limb. "I do remember! You had to boost me up to get me into the tree!"

"You want to go up again?" He grinned and reached for her.

She squealed. "No! I'm not climbing a tree—not in this dress!"

Jeff laughed aloud. "You ought to get a pair of your old overalls on."

"You remember your fourteenth birthday?" she asked, leaning back against the tree and changing the subject.

"I remember every birthday. It's nice we have them on the same day. My fourteenth was the last one before the war began."

"Yes. And I remember you got me a set of paints from the store, and I got you the knife that you'd wanted so long."

Reaching into his pocket, Jeff pulled it out. "Still have it. Cut up quite a few meals with this throughout the war." He opened the blade, which was worn from sharpening. "Sure has been a good one."

"I still have the paints too. I looked at them last night—and at some of the pictures I painted." She giggled. "You should see the ones I painted of you."

"Maybe I shouldn't."

Later, on the way home, he brought up Tom and Sarah.

"Tom hardly ever even speaks to her," Leah said as they came in view of the Carter house.

"I guess he's just afraid that she won't want him."

"He'll never know until he asks, but I *know* she wants him."

73

"Why don't you tell him, Leah?"

"*You* tell him. You're his brother."

"I *have* tried to tell him, but . . . well . . . I don't know. When a fellow's lost a leg, he does feel kind of like a misfit. I can understand how Tom feels."

"He's wrong, though. Sarah didn't fall in love with his leg."

"You're quite an authority on love and romance. You used to read books about them all the time," Jeff teased. "You may be right about this one, though. I know Tom's still in love with her, but besides the problem with the leg, he doesn't have a penny. None of us do."

"That doesn't matter."

"Don't talk foolish!" Jeff said sharply. "Of course, it matters! You've got to have a place to live and food to eat. And don't tell me that God's going to take care of it all. God helps those that help themselves. It says so in the Bible."

Leah waved her hands in exasperation. "It does *not* say that in the Bible! It says that in Aesop's Fables! You know as well as I do—God helps those who *can't* help themselves."

This seemed to strike Jeff as being true. "I know. You're right. So many times during the war when I just couldn't help myself at all, God always saw to it." He smiled at her and took her hand. "You were in some of those escapades." He suddenly lifted her hand, kissed it, and then watched her face.

Leah felt herself blush, but she did not pull her hand back. "Now you're the one who's getting romantic. You practiced up hand kissing with Lucy, I suppose?"

"Now, don't start on Lucy. She and Cecil are going to get married and live happily ever after." He held her hand a moment longer, then said, "Let's go in the house. You can tell me some more about hand kissing later."

Late that night, Sarah was preparing for bed. She was brushing her hair, seated at a dressing table.

Leah watched from her own bed. She asked suddenly, "Has Tom said anything to you?"

Sarah did not miss a stroke. She had beautiful dark hair that came down to her waist and dark blue eyes that looked back at her out of the mirror. She had one of the most beautiful complexions that Leah had ever seen.

"We haven't had a chance to talk much."

"Jeff and I were talking about it. He says Tom is just afraid again to pay you any attention because he lost his leg, and he thinks you've probably changed your mind, and he doesn't have any money. Also, he knows Dewitt Falor's courting you."

"I wish he'd say that to *me*. I could set him straight in a minute."

"Why don't you talk to him?"

"That's not the way it is. A woman can't just go up and start explaining things to a man. He has to say something first."

"I guess so." Leah lay quietly, thinking of the times that she had argued with Jeff. How often she had wanted *him* to speak up and apologize first, knowing at the same time that he was waiting for her to speak. "Life gets complicated, doesn't it?"

"I've never known it to fail. And the older you get, the more complicated it is." Sarah rose, blew out the light, and slipped into bed.

Leah looked out at the half-moon shedding its silvery beams over the apple tree outside their window.

Sarah was silent for a long time. Finally she turned over and faced Leah. "I love him so much! But he's just got to say something to me, Leah."

"I know." Leah yearned to help her sister but did not know how. "We'll just pray, and God will tell him to do it."

"All right. Let's do that. The Bible says if any two people agree that God wants to do something, it'll be done—and you and I agree. So let's pray."

In the silence of the room, the two girls prayed, first for Tom and then for the other family members.

Leah had always felt close to Sarah, and now her heart went out to her sister. After Sarah had gone to sleep, Leah prayed silently, *God, give Tom to Sarah for a husband. Don't let him be foolish and silly.*

Then she turned over and closed her eyes. She thought about the war years that had gone by, and she added another prayer, "And thank You, God, for bringing all our men home safe."

9
Tom Has a Problem

The job of putting the old Turner house into living condition consumed all the energies of the Majorses. Nelson, Tom, and Jeff hauled out trash, mopped floors, cleaned windows—those that were not broken—set up an ancient cookstove by bracing its missing leg with bricks, and worked from sunup to after dark every weekday until May.

One Tuesday morning, Tom thought he was getting up earlier than the others. However, he found Eileen in the kitchen baking bread and said with surprise, "What are you doing up this early?"

"Oh, I just couldn't sleep. Sit down and let me fix you some breakfast."

Taking a chair, Tom looked at his stepmother's face. She looked tired. There were lines around the corners of her mouth that showed strain. "You don't look like you feel well, Eileen. Maybe you better go in and see the doctor."

Eileen reached over and pushed a lock of Tom's hair back from his forehead. "Pooh! Who needs an old doctor? It's only a baby!"

Tom sat sprawled in the chair, his mind going over the day that lay before him.

Eileen soon put eggs and grits before him, then sat down to drink a cup of coffee. "Real coffee tastes good," she said. "I never could get used to drinking coffee made out of burnt acorns."

"I couldn't either," Tom confessed. He sipped the hot brew carefully. "It was nice of the Carters to set us up in groceries—but we can't keep sponging off them forever."

Eileen gave him a quick look. "Things may be hard for a while, but you'll find work."

"That's what I aim to do today. I'm going to walk as far as I can until somebody will hire me to do something. I'm not particular what this time. Just something to bring some cash in."

"Are you going around to the farms or going to town?"

"Both. I'll stop on the farms on the way to town. It's a bad time to be asking for work, especially with so many Union soldiers coming back, but I don't know what else to do, Eileen. Maybe I can get a job cleaning out stables—or just anything."

"You'll find something," Eileen said. "I'll fix a lunch to take with you."

"You don't have to do that."

"You'll need something to eat if you're going to walk all the way to town and back. Some sandwiches, anyway. And I've got two of those doughnuts left."

"Thanks. That would be a help."

By the time Tom left, the sun was coming up over the mountains. He walked as quickly as he could, wishing he had a horse. But there was no money for luxuries like that. By the time he had walked an hour, his leg was beginning to hurt. He looked down at the offending limb and knew that he would never make it to town. Yet he could not turn back. He continued to walk until finally the discomfort became unbearable and he sat down on a fallen tree beside the road.

Half an hour later a wagon came by. Tom looked up hopefully and waved.

"Headed for town, young fella?" The driver was a big, husky man wearing a pair of faded overalls and a straw hat. "Get in and rest your bones!"

"Thanks." Tom climbed awkwardly up onto the wagon seat.

"Hurt your leg, did you?"

Here it comes, Tom thought. *Can't dodge this. I'll just have to tell the truth.* "I lost it at Gettysburg. Confederate army." He looked at the man and waited to be told to get out.

But the man studied him thoughtfully. "Gettysburg, eh? That was a pretty bad fight. I was there myself."

Tom waited for him to continue.

The man grinned. "Actually, I was in the Confederate army myself. Name's Jud Mullins."

Tom took the thick hand that the farmer offered, and a wave of relief washed over him. "I was afraid you were going to say you were Union army and put me out."

"That sort of thing could happen. There're still pretty strong feelings," Mullins said.

"Do you have a farm around here, Mr. Mullins?"

"Yea, a little place. Don't believe I caught your name."

"Tom Majors. My pa and my brother, we all fought. Were in the Stonewall Brigade."

"You tell me that!" Mullins gave him an extra-hard look. "That was the fightingest outfit that I ever heard tell of. I heard old Stonewall liked to walk you fellas to death. Called you his foot cavalry."

"He was a hard man, General Jackson, but a good one."

"So I heard. Fine Christian. Too bad he had to get kilt."

"Jud, do you need any help over on your place? I'm looking for work."

"Well, now, I wish I could say I did. But the truth is, it's just a little place, and the plantin's over, so—"

"Sure, I understand."

The wagon rattled on over the washboard road, with Mullins avoiding such potholes as he could. The two men talked about the war. They had been in many of the same battles. Finally, they came to Pineville.

"I'll be goin' home at about midday, if you want a ride back. Might be a little bit easier on that leg of yours."

"That would be a help, Jud."

"I'll be at the general store about noon. If you're not through, I can maybe wait on you a little bit. It won't take me long to do my business." He grinned, exposing a large gold tooth that glistened in the sun. "Mostly I sit and play checkers and tell lies about the war. You might come on down."

"Might do that, Jud."

Mullins stopped his horses at the edge of the village, and Tom got down. Waving to the friendly farmer, he went into the blacksmith shop where he found Clyde Potter pounding on a horseshoe.

"Hello, Clyde."

"Well, bless my heart if it ain't Tom Majors! I heard you was back!" The burly blacksmith put down his tongs, wiped his hands on his apron, and crunched Tom's hand in a bone-crushing grip. "I'm mighty glad to see you made it."

"Thanks, Clyde. You're still shoeing horses, I see."

Clyde shrugged. "It's about all I know."

"Do you need any help?"

"Did you learn blacksmithing in the army?"

"No, but I've got to learn something. I've got to have work."

Potter scratched his head vigorously. "I wish I could help you, Tom, but there's just not really enough business here for me to take on anybody else. I've got one good hand, and the two of us can handle about all that comes our way."

"You have any idea where I might get work?"

Potter named off a few possibilities, and Tom shook hands with him again and left.

For the next two hours, he went into store after store, omitting none of them except the dress shop. At each place the answer was the same: No help wanted.

Finally, discouraged and tired, Tom sat down on a cane-bottom chair in front of the hardware store and ate the two sandwiches and the doughnuts that Eileen had given him. He was thirsty, and he got a drink from a pump down the street. The water was full of iron, but at least it wet his throat.

Taking a deep breath, he looked up and down, trying to think of another place to go. *I guess I might as well go on home,* he thought.

Just as he passed one of the town's three saloons, the batwing doors suddenly burst open, and he was almost pushed off the sidewalk into the street. He caught his balance by grabbing one of the uprights supporting the shed roof that covered the walk.

"Why don't you watch where you're going, Reb?"

Instantly Tom grew alert. He turned to find the two men who had just exited watching him in a strange manner. He knew both of them. Buck

Noland and Arlo Simms were typical town no-goods. They worked when they had to, drank when they could get liquor, and fought for no reason.

Noland was a broad man with pale hair. He surveyed Tom for a moment and said, "I heard you was back from the war. I guess we whipped up on you Rebels, didn't we?"

"You were in the army?" Tom asked innocently, knowing that Noland had used every trick in the book to stay out.

"None of your business!" Noland said. Then he grinned. "Arlo, here's a good example of that Southern white trash we whipped up on. Ain't much, is he?"

Arlo Simms was as tall and thin as Buck Noland was thick and strong. He had a pair of pale hazel eyes and a wide mouth, almost like a catfish's. "He ain't much at that, Buck!" Stepping closer, Simms said, "I said you wasn't much, Reb. What you gonna do about it?"

The two men obviously wanted trouble, and Tom swiftly decided to avoid them. "I'm not going to do anything except go home."

He started down the walk, but Noland grabbed him with a thick arm. "I'll tell you what, Reb," he said. "I'm gonna take you in the saloon and buy you a drink, and you're going to drink to General Ulysses S. Grant, and you're gonna cuss Robert E. Lee and Jackson and all that trash."

"Let go of my arm, Noland!"

But Tom had little chance. The two men bracketed him at once and dragged him into the saloon. At once Tom saw Dewitt Falor at the bar, and again the alarms went off. *Falor put them up to it,* he thought.

"Hey, looky what we got here, Dewitt," Noland said, smirking. He kept his hold on Tom's arm as did Simms on the other. "We got us a Rebel here. He don't look so tough to me."

Tom knew Falor only slightly. He was two years younger than Tom, and his father owned immense land tracts as well as some of the businesses in town. Falor was a rather bulky man with tow hair and close-set brown eyes. He was wearing expensive clothes. There was a whiskey bottle on the bar in front of him, half empty.

"Well, now," Falor said, grinning, "you fellows done captured yourself a prisoner. How you doing, Majors?"

Tom was gripped so firmly by the men that he knew that only by putting up a tremendous struggle would he get loose—which was exactly what they wanted. He said quietly, "Hello, Falor. If you'll tell your friends here to turn loose of me, I'll just get out of your way."

"No, you're going to have a drink," Noland said. "Pour some whiskey out there, Dewitt. Majors here is going to drink to General Grant."

Falor said with surprise that was obviously an act. "Is he now? Then I guess he's been converted."

"That ain't all," Arlo Simms said. "He's gonna cuss Robert E. Lee and Jackson."

"I'm glad to hear it," Falor said. He poured some whiskey into a glass and held it out. "Here you go. You can drink to Grant first and cuss Lee later."

"I don't want to drink."

Falor's eyes grew cold and hard.

Everybody in Pineville was aware of Tom's interest in Sarah Carter. And Falor was used to getting what he wanted. Maybe, Tom thought, he saw his chance to strike a blow at an adversary.

"You're gonna drink this," he said.

"No, I'm not!" Tom struggled to get free and found his arms clapped tightly together. "Turn me loose," he said, "or we'll have trouble."

Falor dashed the glass of raw alcohol into his eyes.

Tom gasped with pain and was forced to shut his eyes.

Falor drew back his fist and landed a staggering right that caught Tom in the mouth. He was knocked backward, torn from the grip of Simms and Noland, and he tasted blood where his teeth had cut his lip. He was struggling blindly to get up when he heard Falor say, "Bust him up, fellas. Teach him what it means to be a Rebel."

Tom fought as best he could, but the situation was hopeless. He was still half blinded by the whiskey and stunned by the vicious blow he had taken. Simms's and Noland's fists struck him repeatedly in the face and in the body, and, though he tried to fight back, Tom soon sensed himself slipping away. And then he felt himself being lifted and dragged across the room.

"Throw him out of here!" Falor's voice seemed to come from a long way off.

Somebody pitched Tom through the front doors. He hit the wooden sidewalk and rolled out into the dirt of the street.

Half conscious, he was struggling to get to his feet when he felt a strong hand on his arm.

"Come along, Tom." It was the voice of Jud Mullins.

Falor and his two friends stepped outside and looked at the big farmer. "That trash a friend of yours?"

"You might say so, although I just met him. Come along, Tom," he repeated.

"Maybe we ought to bust him up too. He's another Reb," Noland said and took one step forward.

He stopped abruptly, however, for from beneath his clothing Jud Mullins produced an enormous .44 and held it directly on Noland.

"Hey, now! I ain't got no gun!"

"I have," Jud Mullins said. "You got anything else to say?"

"No. No," Noland said grimly. He turned and went back into the saloon.

Jud Mullins said to the other two, "You better join your friend. This gun don't work very good. It goes off sometimes by accident."

Arlo Simms whirled and dived into the saloon.

Falor stayed just a moment to give the farmer a hard look, but his words were to Tom. "I wouldn't make it a habit of comin' to town. We don't need Rebels here. Why don't you go back down South where you belong?" He turned and walked inside.

Tom found himself half carried to Jud's wagon. The farmer helped him onto the seat, where he tried to clean the blood off his face with trembling hands.

Mullins spoke to the horses, and the wagon moved. When they were out of town, he said quietly, "Not everybody in this town is like those three. I wouldn't judge Pineville by them."

Tom was too nauseated to speak. He simply nodded and for the rest of the way home thought only of how he could keep his father from hearing about what had happened. There would be trouble. On the other hand, he knew it would be impossible to keep such news. Pineville loved its gossip.

He thought grimly, *Everyone in the county will know a Majors got beat up by Dewitt Falor.*

10
The Courting

As the Majors family settled down into their rather precarious shack, the most exciting activities around Pineville seemed to be the courtship of two couples.

Actually, both Royal and Rosie were taken by surprise. Each young man considered that he had already done a sufficient amount of courting back in Tennessee. They were soon, however, enlightened by their prospective brides.

Rosie was the first to discover that he had not fulfilled Charlie's expectation of what a young man should do. He'd come out to the Carter house several times and sat on the front porch with his fiancée. Then suddenly, one evening after supper, the roof seemed to fall in on him.

Rosie had managed to devour a large part of a huge turkey, alternating huge bites of the delicious white and dark meat with complaints of how easily his stomach got upset. Staggering out to the front porch afterward, he collapsed into a cane-bottom rocker.

He was joined almost at once by Charlene Satterfield. She sat in a chair beside him and listened to him moan about his health for some time, but she said nothing. She was an attractive girl, especially now that she had learned to wear dresses. When Drake and Rosie had first met her in Atlanta, she had dressed like a man, having been raised much like a boy.

Tonight Charlie wore an apricot-colored dress that Lori had helped her with. Her hair was carefully arranged, and obviously she had gone to great lengths to make herself as pretty as possible.

Rosie turned his head and looked at her. "What's the matter, Charlie? You're not saying anything."

"How can I say anything?" Charlie said. "You're groaning like a pig that's eaten too much corn."

"Well, that was a good supper. I just hope it don't discombobulate my digestion." He looked over again and said, "You seem out of sorts. Are you feeling peaked?"

"I feel fine!" Charlie's voice, however, was sharp, and suddenly she turned on him. "You may as well go on home if all you're going to do is sit there and groan!"

Her sudden anger took Rosie off guard. Charlie Satterfield was one of the best tempered girls he had ever met, which was one reason he wanted to marry her. He straightened up and said, "I can tell you're upset. What is it? Tell old Rosie—he'll fix it."

Suddenly Charlie was on her feet. "All right! I'll tell you! All you've done since you got back from the army is come here and eat and set on this porch!" She was almost crying.

Rosie rose to his feet. He was very fond of this young woman. He put a hand on her shoulder. "Well, now, dog my cats!" he muttered. "Something's wrong. Just tell me what it is."

Charlie looked up at him. "I'll tell you what's wrong! You treat me like a piece of furniture, not like a woman!"

"What's that you say?"

"You never dress up to come out and see me. You never notice when I put on a new dress, or

88

when I fix my hair. You never say anything roman-tic to me. You just don't treat me like a woman."

She wheeled and left the porch. "And don't call me Charlie," she shouted back. "My name is Charlene!"

"Well—hey, now—" Rosie sputtered feebly. Be-wildered by the broadsides he had just received, he followed her into the house.

"Where's Charlie—I mean, where's Charlene?" he asked.

Lori and Royal were sitting on the couch in the parlor. Lori said, "She went upstairs. She's crying. What did you say to her?"

"I didn't say *anything* to her. Not a word."

"I expect that's right!" Lori said in disgust.

Royal, who had been leaning back with a hand behind his head and his legs stretched out, looked as though the meal had stupefied him too. He straightened up. "What did you do to her?"

"Why, I was just sittin' there tellin' her about studyin' how to keep a stomach in good condition," Rosie said pitifully, "and she jumped all over me like a duck on a June bug! She said I wasn't roman-tic and all I did was come here and eat like a pig and then groan."

"I think that describes you pretty well, Rosie," Royal said.

Lori stood. "And you might take some of those same criticisms to yourself, Royal Carter!" She stalked from the room, saying, "I'm going to see if I can comfort Charlene. You two can romance each other. All you do is eat anyway!"

Rosie and Royal stared at each other.

Finally Royal said, "Well, I guess the fat's in the fire now. What did you have to make Charlie so mad for?"

"I didn't make her mad on purpose!" Rosie said defensively. "What did you make Lori mad for?"

Royal scratched his head. "You know, maybe they're right. I thought we'd done all the courting we needed to do back in Tennessee. We proposed and everything."

"Well, I can see right now that won't do it. We got to do something, Royal."

"But what?"

"We got to court those girls proper. Get some Macassar oil to put on our hair. Get some stiff white collars." Rosie stretched his imagination. "We got to get some guitars and stand out under their winders and sing songs to 'em—romantic songs."

"I won't do it!" Royal growled.

Rosie never got his guitar, but from that moment the two boys did make it a point to be more attentive to the young ladies.

For three days they put forth their best efforts. They rented a carriage and took the girls over to the next small town, where there was a visiting orchestra (which Rosie thought played "just plumb awful"). Rosie brought flowers for Charlene—she demanded that he call her that—and after a time the couples seemed to be back on an even track.

It was a Tuesday afternoon. Jeff and Royal came by to see Rosie in his hotel room and found him getting ready to call on Charlene.

"You're going to have to get yourself a claw-hammer coat, Rosie," Jeff told his tall, gangling friend.

Royal laughed at Rosie's expression. "That's right. You need to dress up like an undertaker or a deacon."

"I always heard that clothes don't make the man," Rosie protested.

"I always heard that fine feathers made fine birds." Royal grinned. "Now you look at me. I bought this suit especially for courting Lori, and I suppose I'll have to have another one to get married in. No telling what a fellow will do when he falls in love, is there?"

When Rosie was ready, they went downstairs. They were met at the bottom of the steps by the clerk, who said, "Hey, Jeff. Did you hear about Tom?"

"Tom? You mean my brother?"

"Yeah, I mean your brother! Who else would I be talking about?" the clerk said impatiently. "You didn't hear about it?"

"What's happened?" Jeff saw the excitement in the man's eyes and could not imagine what was going on.

"He got all beat up," the clerk said.

"*Beat up?* Who did it? When did it happen?"

"Why, not more than an hour ago. He come to town, Tom did, and he run across Buck Noland and Arlo Simms at the saloon. The way I hear it, Tom was plumb drunk, and he jumped on Simms, and Noland had to jump in and take his part. And then he took a swing at Dewitt Falor too. I expect you better get home. He didn't look too good, some of the fellas said that saw it."

"Come on," Royal said angrily, "we'd better find out about this!"

Falor, Simms, and Noland were in the saloon drinking.

91

Royal walked over to their table and said, "What's this about a fight between you and Tom Majors?"

"He a friend of yours?" Falor asked.

"Yes, he is! Now, what about it?"

"He thinks he's a bully boy," Falor said. "He came in here and started cussin' General Grant and the Union army. We tried to quiet him down, and he swung on me. We had to throw him out. I reckon he was drunk, Royal."

Jeff stepped up, his dark eyes flashing. "You're a liar! Tom doesn't drink, but I see you do!"

"Get this kid out of here, Royal! You and Rosie ought to know better than to bring an innocent boy like this into a saloon."

"I'm old enough to be in a saloon! I just don't want to be here with clowns like you!"

Buck Noland stood up. "We whipped one Majors today. I guess we can whip another one."

Rosie—tall, strong, and rather dangerous-looking at the moment—put a hand on Buck Noland's chest and shoved.

Noland went reeling back into his chair, which tipped over. He scrambled to his feet, clenching both of his huge fists. He stopped as he saw Rosie's eyes light up for battle. "What part you got in this, Rosie? He ain't no kinfolk to you, is he?"

"You was too much of a coward to fight on either side of the war, Buck Noland!" Rosie said mildly. "If you don't shut your mouth, I'll have to shut it for you! I may do it anyway!"

"What really went on here?" Royal asked.

"I told you how it was!" Falor said. "And more than that, he was makin' light with your sister's name. Wasn't he, fellas?"

The two nodded. "Sure was."

Falor said, "I couldn't stand for that. You know how I feel about Sarah."

"Come on," Jeff said. "He's a liar down to his boots. Tom would never say anything bad about Sarah, and you know it!"

Royal hesitated for just a moment. "I'm going to get to the bottom of this, Dewitt. But let me tell you one thing—the next time you lay a hand on Tom, you might as well try to lay one on me too. And that goes for you other two yahoos!"

Royal whirled and walked out the door, followed by his two friends. They went to his wagon, and he drove the horses toward home at a speed that must have astonished the poor beasts.

At the Carters', all three jumped out and ran toward the house.

Tom was lying on the couch, his eyes almost closed, his lips puffy. Sarah sat beside him, bathing his face. She glanced up as Royal and Jeff and Rosie hurried in.

Jeff came straight to his brother's side. "We heard the lies that Dewitt told. What was the truth of it?"

Tom tried to sit up, but Sarah said, "You stay right down there, Tom Majors!" She turned on Royal. "And where were *you*, Royal? Why didn't you help him?"

Defensively, Royal threw his hands up. "We didn't know a thing about it, sis! Not until we were coming out of the hotel room."

"How was it, Tom?" Rosie demanded. "All we heard was some big windy tale from Falor and his friends."

Tom once again attempted to sit up, but Sarah held a hand on his head so that he couldn't move. "You three get out of here and go about your business!"

"But, sis—" Royal protested.

Sarah felt she had no patience left. *"Get out, I said!"*

"Well, all right. We'll wait outside, but we want to talk to you when you get to feeling better, Tom."

She watched them leave, then turned back to Tom. She dipped the cloth into the cool water and bathed his face once more.

"I feel like such a fool," Tom groaned. "Went through five years of the war, and now they beat me up like I was a kid."

"Lie still." Sarah leaned over and looked at his eyebrow. "You really ought to have some stitches in that."

"No, it'll be all right. Just let it alone."

Sarah sat quietly beside him. It was the first time she had been alone with Tom since he had come home. Finally she said, "It looks like you had to get yourself whipped before I would have a chance to talk to you, Tom."

"What do you mean? We talk every day."

"No, we don't. We just make noises. You haven't said one real thing to me, Tom Majors, since you came home from the war!"

"Well, I—"

"You hush! I'm talking now!" Sarah put her face directly in front of his. "I've seen you run from me one time too many, and I want to know one thing, Tom Majors . . ." She swallowed hard, then said strongly, "All those times that you came out here and told me that you loved me—it must've been

94

fifty times before the war—were those all lies, Tom?"

Astonished, he sat up. He swayed, struggling to see her through his puffy eyes. "Lies? No, they weren't lies!"

"Then you loved me before the war?"

"Of course I did."

"But you don't love me now?"

"I never said that," he murmured.

"You haven't said *anything!* All you've done is run from me ever since you've gotten here! What am I supposed to think?"

Tom bowed his head. "I guess," he said finally, "you're supposed to think that I don't have anything to offer you, Sarah. I'm a cripple and don't have a dime!" Bitterness drew his lips into a tight line. "Besides, what about Dewitt Falor? What am I supposed to think about him?"

"Dewitt Falor's interest is all one-sided—his *side!* I'd have told you that if you had ever asked me! I've been waiting five years for *you*." She spoke more softly. "You went away and fought for the cause you believed in and gave part of yourself for it. I admired you for doing that, even though I thought your cause was wrong. But now there's something I don't admire. If you loved me, you'd do whatever you had to do to get me. That's what a man does who loves a woman!"

Tom reached out and took her shoulders. "Sarah!" His voice was intense, and he held her for one moment, looking into her eyes. "I still love you like I always have." He swallowed hard and said, "I haven't got a thing to offer you, but will you marry me?"

Sarah's lips turned up. "I'll marry you."

And then he kissed her.

When he lifted his head, she said archly, "I'll marry you, but you're going to have to come courting, just like Rosie and Royal are doing!"

"Oh, Sarah, I love you so much, I'll even get a guitar and sing songs under your window."

"No, don't do that! You'd scare the chickens."

11
Another War

I can't help worrying, Eileen."

Nelson Majors and his wife were sitting in their almost bare living room. It had only a few scattered pieces of furniture to adorn it. They had done their best with the house, but it was still a shack. It was so weakly constructed, in fact, that Nelson and Tom and Jeff had cut saplings to brace it on the north side where it threatened to collapse. In some places, the boards had shrunk so that birds could fly through the cracks. Jeff fought a never-ending battle against the rats that were inhabiting the place when they moved in. And the attic proved to be full of bats, which frightened Eileen.

She had never made a single complaint. She had kept herself cheerful, though she was not feeling well. "It'll be all right, Nelson," she said now. "You'll find work soon."

"No work and no future." His voice was filled with gloom.

Tom and Jeff's father was by nature a cheerful man, but the incessant struggle to find a better place for his child to be born was weighing heavily upon him. Dan Carter had told him again and again to trust God. He knew that was what he must do. He had spent hours working on the old house but also many hours out in the woods, simply walking and praying.

As much as possible, he was on the move looking for work. He had been an engineer in the army, but there was little call for engineers in Pineville. He had thought at one time he had a good chance to work for the railroad, laying new tracks. But when this called for him to leave Kentucky and go to the far West, he had to decline.

Eileen put her hand on his. "It's not too late for you to take that job with the railroad."

"No, I couldn't do that. I've got to be here when the baby comes."

She squeezed his hand. "I'll be all right. You do what you think you need to do."

Nelson was tempted, but he knew he could not do it. He held her close, saying, "We'll make out somehow. I'll go hunting tomorrow. There's some fat deer over in the bottomland by the river. We won't starve anyway. But I didn't have in mind bringing you to a place like this, Eileen. A man wants to do better than this for his family."

Leah and Jeff stopped at the edge of the ravine and stood panting.

A bright sun looked through the scattered clouds, casting down its beams. Jeff removed his hat and wiped his brow with a red bandanna. "Sure is hot for May," he said.

"It certainly is." Leah had, at Jeff's request, found a pair of overalls that had belonged to her brother, Royal. She had donned a light, pale green shirt and wore a straw hat that covered her blonde hair, except for tendrils that escaped from time to time. Stuffing the curls back under the hat, she said, "I know why you wanted to come here, Jeff."

"Sure, I wanted to see the old home place." He stood looking down into the small valley below. The house seemed to have been made to nestle inside the bend of the creek that half circled it. On the north side was lush pastureland with cows grazing placidly in the soft, green spring grass. Farther on and to the west, the mountains rose, but not before plowed fields gave back the sun's heat to the skies.

"Sure is a pretty place," Jeff murmured. "Pa built that house himself. I was only three years old, but I remember getting in his way trying to help."

"It is a pretty place."

They stood silently gazing down at the old homestead. It appeared to have been recently painted.

Then Jeff murmured, "I remember Ma made Pa fix those shutters. Then we got into a fight about what color to paint them. I wanted orange, and they laughed at me for that."

"Who picked out the blue color?"

"Ma did. Pretty, isn't it?"

"Yes, it is." A longing came over Leah, and she wanted to say something like, "I wish you still lived there," but she knew that would only hurt Jeff. Instead, she said, "Look, there's Thunder."

"By george, you're right!" Thunder had been one of his father's prize horses. They had sold the animal to the Joneses, when they bought the farm. "He still looks good. Tom used to win some races on him. Good old Thunder."

As if he had heard the boy's voice, the bay lifted his head and pawed at the dirt, then broke into a run. Leah could hear the sound of his hoofs, like miniature thunder, even high on the hill where they stood.

Jeff said, "I'd sure like to throw a saddle on him and ride him hard and fast about as far as I could get."

Not wanting him to become sad, Leah said, "Why don't we go down to the creek now?"

"We didn't bring any lines to fish with."

"I know, but maybe we can catch a turtle or something."

"I think it's the funniest thing I ever saw," Lori said, looking out the window.

Royal came up beside her. "Why? It's only Rosie."

"I know, but look what he's got with him."

Royal grinned. "I know. He's brought Charlie's wedding present."

"You must call her Charlene now. She's a grown lady." Then she called out, "Charlene! Your fiancé is here!"

A door slammed down the hall, and Charlene quickly appeared.

"He's out front, and he's got something you're going to like," Lori said.

Rosie stood in front of the Carter house with a set of matched blue-nosed mules, tall and strong-looking. One suddenly made a wild bite at his shoulder. He leaned back, avoiding the heavy teeth, and whacked the mule across the nose. "Stop that! Do you hear me?"

Wonderingly, Charlene came close to the huge animals. She reached up and stroked the nearest one's nose. "Oh, Rosie, they're the most beautiful mules I ever saw. Every bit as pretty as the pair I had back in Georgia."

"Well, they're kind of a weddin' present, you might say. A little bit early, but I thought we might hitch 'em up and see how they do."

"Let's go right now!"

"Wait a minute!" Rosie said in alarm. "You can't plow in that pretty dress! I'll tell you what—you let me do the plowing, and you do the watching."

"No! Well . . . all right for now. Come on, Rosie!" She grabbed his arm, and the two led the mules almost at a run toward the open field.

Inside the house, Royal and Lori were laughing heartily at Charlene's excitement.

"I never thought a woman could get so excited about a pair of ugly mules," Royal said, sitting on the couch.

Lori sat down beside him. "They're not ugly to her. She loves mules."

"I think they're going to have their farm and everything ready by the time they get married. You know, I thought Rosie was kind of a slowpoke, but when he gets going he is really something. Here he bought himself a farm, got him some blue-nosed mules, got him a bride picked out. He's all set."

They were interrupted then as Tom and Sarah came in. They had been in the kitchen, making lemonade, and Sarah carried four glasses on a tray. "Here, try some of this," she said. "It's not cold, but it's wet."

The two couples drank lemonade and laughed about the mules. Then Tom said, "Royal and Lori, Sarah and I've been talking. What would you say if we had a double wedding? We'll all be in the family."

"Oh, that would be wonderful!" Lori said.

"It'll save money too." Royal winked across the

room at Tom. "We won't have to pay the preacher but one fee!"

"You are awful, Royal!" Sarah said.

"Well, every penny counts, but I think it's a great idea."

After a while Sarah said, "Why don't we go to town right now, Lori, and see if we can find some material for our wedding dresses—if the men will take us."

"Wonderful!"

And soon a buggy was on the way to Pineville.

"I never thought anyone could be so happy," Sarah whispered to Tom. They were in the backseat, and he had his arm around her. "I'm the happiest girl in the world."

"No, you're not!" Lori turned around and grinned. "I am!"

A small argument took place over this, and finally the girls agreed that they were equally happy.

Shopping trips in Pineville did not usually take long. There were only three stores that would have anything like wedding dress material.

For a time, Tom and Royal stood looking on as the young women apparently had to examine every bolt. Once Tom made a suggestion, saying, "I kind of like that," but he was at once shouted down.

"That ugly thing! I wouldn't wear that to a dog-fight!" Sarah said indignantly. "You two go somewhere and entertain yourselves. Come back in about an hour or two."

"I think that's a good idea," Royal said.

The men went to the blacksmith shop and watched the farrier shoe horses for a while, an operation that always fascinated Tom.

They had just left and started down the street when Dewitt Falor appeared out of nowhere. He saw them and headed in their direction, his head thrust forward and his eyes hot with anger.

"He's spoiling for a fight, Tom," Royal said. "Let's get out of here."

"I can't spend the rest of my life running from Dewitt Falor."

"You can't fight him either."

"Why can't I?"

"He's a no-good, spoiled, rich brat, but he's smart. He wouldn't come at us this way unless he had a plan."

As if by accident, other men began to gather round as Falor strolled toward them. Some of them Tom knew.

"There's Buck Noland and Arlo Simms. They're wanting to beat me up again, I guess. Maybe they'll hold me while Falor does the job."

There were at least a half dozen others in the crowd.

When Falor stood in front of him, Tom said, "I don't want any trouble with you, Dewitt. I just came to town for my fiancée to do some shopping."

At the mention of Sarah, Falor's face flushed. He had always been able to get everything he wanted—except Sarah Carter. Tom well knew that he had been boasting around town that he might have lost Sarah but her bridegroom was going have to pay for her with blood.

A shifty-eyed man Tom had never seen before said, "Why don't you Rebels just go back where you come from?"

A murmur of agreement ran around. Visibly encouraged by it, the man began to curse the South.

The chorus was taken up by others. Someone shoved Tom, and Royal said, "Dewitt, call these bums off!"

"Who you callin' a bum?"

Somebody struck Royal in the face. It was a wild, wicked blow, and he flew backwards.

Tom swung from the heels, catching directly the nose of the man who had hit Royal. Blood spurted, and the man uttered a howl before he fell.

Buck Noland said, "Get 'em!" and the men surged forward.

For a brief time, Tom and Royal did well, but the weight of numbers soon wore them down. Royal managed to put another one of the attackers on his back, but then two more men joined the fray.

"We've got to run for it!" Royal cried.

"No." Tom gritted his teeth. "I'm not running anymore!" He took a blow high on the temple that half spun him around. He turned back to see that it was Dewitt Falor who had struck him. "What about just you and me, Dewitt? That's what this is all about."

"Me fight you? Why, sure. That's what I wanted all the time."

"What's going on here?"

The men all turned to see Rosie and Drake Bedford running across the street. Drake was a known fighter, and Rosie was his equal. The odds had suddenly shifted.

Rosie took the burly Noland by the shirt collar. "I'm gonna have to disconnect you, I reckon. You don't learn no other way."

"Wait a minute!" Tom's heart warmed to see who had come to his side. He looked across at Drake and Rosie and said, "We fought on different sides, fellas . . ."

"I know that," Drake said carelessly, "but I always had respect for you Confederates." He glanced at Simms and Noland. "Unlike these snakes here. Nobody could respect them! I think we better begin to proceed to commence to wipe up the deck with 'em."

"No," Tom said quickly. "I appreciate you fellas coming to help, but this is between me and Falor."

"That's right," Falor said quickly. He was a tall, thickset man with strong-looking shoulders, although he had developed a fairly large stomach. Tom had an artificial leg, and Falor outweighed him by at least thirty pounds. "Let's us have it out right here and now! We'll see who the best man is! I'll put you in such shape you won't get married for six months!"

"All right. Just you and me then, Falor."

Tom stepped into the street, and Falor followed. Immediately a ring of men encircled them.

Falor cried, "I'm gonna bust you up! You stole my girl!" He threw a huge fist that would have ended the fight right then had it landed.

But Tom simply moved his head to one side, and as Falor went by, off balance from the force of the blow, he pivoted and struck the huge man in the small of the back.

Falor turned around, his face contorted. He took a deep breath and threw himself straight at Tom again.

Rather than being wrestled to the ground by the heavier man, Tom slipped by and struck him directly in the throat.

It was a well-aimed, hard blow. Falor suddenly seemed unable to breathe. Grasping his throat, he began to gag, and the men in the circle looked stunned at the ease with which Tom had stopped the big man.

"That's enough of this, Dewitt," Tom said. "No sense fighting. We're going to be living in this town a long time. Are you willing to shake hands and start all over again?"

Falor probably was not willing but was in pain from his beaten kidney and still could barely speak. His friends were staring at him with disbelief. Tom's friends were staring at *him* with wide grins.

Falor suddenly reached out, pressed the hand Tom offered, and croaked, "All right, I guess." Then he wheeled and made his way down the street, weaving slightly.

"I guess you done the necessary, Tom," Rosie said. "I don't figure you're going to have any more trouble with him or his kind."

"I probably will," Tom said. "The war made some deep hurts, and we're going to have to learn to work through them."

"I guess if fellas like us that fought on different sides can make up, everybody else can do the same," Drake said.

Rosie added, "You ought to ask Falor to the wedding."

"Anybody can come to the wedding. And inviting him special would just make him mad all over again," Tom said. "I actually feel sorry for the fella. I know how I'd feel if Sarah had chosen him instead of me."

"Come on, let's go have a look at the brides," Rosie said. "They ought to have bought enough material to make a covered wagon by now."

The four friends, who had lately been on different sides of the great conflict, joined arms and started down the street.

All of Pineville watched as three Yankees and a Rebel paraded their loyalty to one another. Those who hated the South knew that they had seen something that they had never expected to see. Some would not accept it. But others, seeing the young men who had fought in both blue and gray, looked at each other and said, "I believe something is going to happen to this country yet. Something good!"

12
Made in Heaven

The church was decorated with peach blossoms and wild flowers. Someone had obtained yellow-and-white streamers and festooned these from the high ceiling. Every seat in the auditorium was taken, and some spectators stood outside looking in the windows as the minister entered from the rear of the church with Tom and Royal on either side of him.

Tom was wearing a dark blue suit with a white shirt and string tie. Royal wore black with ruffles at the throat of his white shirt. A pair of shiny black boots peeped out from beneath the trousers.

"They look like they're about to run," Jeff whispered to his father, sitting beside him on the front row.

"That's the way you're supposed to feel when you get married." Nelson Majors winked. "No, not really, Jeff. They're both going to be happy couples."

As Jeff looked back, he saw Esther coming down the aisle next, carrying a basket of flowers. Leah and Sarah had made her a frilly white dress. She was smiling broadly, and she waved at Jeff as she passed. "Hello, Jeff," she said. "I'm the flower girl."

A twitter went over the church, but the beauty of the child charmed them all.

Jeff looked back again. Leah was coming. She was wearing a white dress trimmed with lace at the neck and sleeves. The V-shaped bodice was tight fitting, and narrow pink satin ribbon ran from the high neckline to meet at the point of the V at the waist. The full skirt was trimmed with lace and embroidered pink flowers.

Jeff could hardly believe his eyes. This beautiful young woman was the girl he had thrown into the creek more than once, the one he had hunted possums with. He held his breath as she passed by.

She smiled at him. There was something mysterious and wise in her expression, and Jeff swallowed hard. He whispered to his father, "Leah sure looks good, doesn't she?"

"She's a beautiful woman, Jeff," his father answered quietly.

And then the two brides came in, side by side.

Both girls wore white satin gowns with neat, high necklines and close-fitting embroidered bodices. Their skirts were very full and lace trimmed. Sarah had on a white straw hat decorated with orange blossoms and wild flowers and a dainty lace veil that draped to her shoulders. Lori wore a white satin pillbox trimmed with a sprig of orange blossom. Her short veil was of the same dainty material. Both wore white gloves and satin shoes and carried orange blossom bouquets.

When they reached the front of the church, the minister said, "You gentlemen may each take the hand of your bride."

Afterward, neither Tom nor Royal could remember much about the ceremony except how beautiful his bride looked.

When the ceremony had ended and they had kissed the brides and fled from the church, Leah joined Jeff. "Wasn't that the most beautiful wedding you ever saw?"

"Just about. I don't ever remember two better-looking couples," he said.

Eileen had been standing close enough to hear Jeff's comment, and she whispered to her husband, "I can think of another good-looking couple."

"You mean Jeff and Leah?"

"Yes, that's exactly right."

"Someday maybe. Not for a while."

The reception was in the nature of a feast, and the church ladies and other friends of the Majorses and the Carters had outdone themselves. There were no tiny glasses of punch. There were no fragile china plates with small squares of cake. Instead there was a full-fledged wedding supper.

Tom and Royal had to endure endless torment on the part of their old comrades, who teased them unmercifully. Sarah and Lori happily escaped much of this.

And then, suddenly, there was a commotion at the front of the reception room. When Tom turned, he saw to his dismay Dewitt Falor coming through the crowd.

Oh, no! he thought. *Not a fight! Not here at my wedding!*

Falor planted his feet firmly in front of Tom and stopped.

Silence fell over the room. It felt as if everyone was standing on tiptoe to see what would happen. Pineville loved its drama, and here it was. One man had lost, and another had won. Now the loser had come to settle scores!

"Hello, Dewitt," Tom said.

"Hello, Tom."

Rosie edged closer, looking around, presumably for Falor's friends. However, the man seemed to be alone.

Tom saw that Falor had an odd look on his face, a look he could not identify. "I'm glad you came, Dewitt."

"I almost didn't." Falor stared at the floor and shifted his feet. Finally he looked up, and his face was red. "I guess . . . well, I guess I got to do something I never thought I'd do."

Rosie and Jeff moved closer.

"I guess I got to tell you," Falor said slowly, "that I been wrong about everything."

A mutter went over the crowd, as people murmured in amazement. Dewitt Falor never apologized to anybody. Everyone knew that.

Falor's eyes went to Sarah. "I didn't come to spoil your wedding, Sarah, or your reception. But since I done Tom wrong in public, I felt that it was only fair that I come and apologize in public."

Sarah put out her hand, and when Falor took it with some embarrassment, she smiled sweetly. "That's very decent of you, Dewitt. Thank you. I'm so glad you came." She squeezed his hand and said, "It's a very wonderful thing your coming like this. Not many men would have had the courage to do it." Then she added, "Someday some woman's going to get a fine husband."

Relief washed over Dewitt Falor's face. He grunted and said, "Well . . . I guess I better go."

"No sense going," Tom said quickly. "Come and have some of this food. Plenty left."

Later—after both couples had departed for some mysterious spot that they would not name to anyone, and the wedding guests had dispersed—Jeff and Leah walked the deserted street, talking about what had happened.

Jeff had been thinking about the strangeness of it all. "You could've knocked me over with a feather when Dewitt apologized. I always thought he was no good to the core, but I guess he's got some good in him after all."

"I think he has. It's like Sarah said," Leah murmured. "It took a lot of courage to come out in public and apologize."

"Anyway, I'm glad it's over. Now he and Tom won't be walking around each other, ready for a fight every time they meet. Tom doesn't need that."

"No, he doesn't." Leah took his arm, and they walked slowly the length of the street, then back. "Both families and Drake and Rosie are going to have a snack at our house before Tom and Sarah and Royal and Lori leave on their honeymoons."

"Who needs more food? Besides, they'll be too nervous to eat," Jeff said with a grin. "And I don't blame them. I would be too!"

"Well, you're not getting married, so you can eat all you want to. Come on, Jeff! I've got to help get the food ready."

13
Happy Ending

The Carter house was bursting at its seams. All the Carters were there, of course—Mr. and Mrs. Carter and Leah and Morena, Leah's young sister, plus Uncle Silas. The Majors families were jammed up to the table too. Nelson and Eileen sat together; Jeff held Esther on his lap across from them. And the newlywed couples were seated beside each other.

The bridegrooms had been too nervous to eat at first, but finally they managed to make a good enough showing.

Leah and Jeff sat together. Jeff now and again cast a look at the young woman beside him, unable to believe that this was the girl whose hook he'd had to bait with a worm.

Leah dropped her eyes demurely when he glanced her direction.

And then Dan Carter tapped on his water glass with a spoon. When he had everyone's attention, he said, "I've eaten too much to make a speech at this family gathering. Nelson, I'm going to ask you to do the honors."

Nelson rose to his feet. He looked around, and a silence fell across the room. "I'm thinking," he said, "about a meal we had here five years ago. It was when the war came, and we were divided—as were so many neighbors in this country. I went South to Virginia and joined the Confederacy, along with my sons. Others stayed here."

113

Nelson's eyes lighted on Royal and Rosie and Drake, and his voice grew even quieter. "Somehow a miracle has taken place. God has kept every one of us safe, and I believe we ought to thank Him for it."

As his father bowed his head and gave thanks for the grace of God, Jeff was surprised to feel Leah suddenly grasp his hand and squeeze it so hard it almost hurt. He stole a glance at her and saw that tears were trickling down her cheeks. He himself felt somewhat misty-eyed.

When he ended the prayer, Nelson said, "And how does a man find the words to thank his neighbors when they practically save his life? If it hadn't been for you, Dan and Mary, I don't know what would have become of little Esther there. She's become almost like one of your own, I know, and I thank you from the bottom of my heart. I thank you for all you've done for my family. For welcoming us back after the war when many would not have done so."

He paused, then said, "There are only so many ways to say thank you, and I wish I knew them all. But you must know this, that in my heart I will never forget what the Carters have done for the Majorses."

As soon as he sat down, Dan Carter rose, looking around the table. "I can only say this—we've just done what we could, and I know that the Majorses would have done as much for us."

There was a slight ripple of applause, and Dan held up his hands. "Now I've got an announcement to make. All of you know what a mean, stubborn man I am."

A groan went up, and there was much head shaking.

"It's true," Dan said. "I may not show it, but I get downright stubborn. I just want my own way sometimes."

"Amen to that!" Mrs. Carter snapped, but she was laughing at her husband.

"Mary knows it's true. Well, I've decided to have my own way." His eyes rested on the Majors family. "I like to choose my own neighbors. Now, you take the Joneses that bought your old place. I suppose they're all right, but they're clannish folk. All stick together. Haven't done well with that farm, either. Lost money on it every year. Takes real talent to lose money on a good farm like you left 'em, Nelson, but that's exactly what they've done."

Dan Carter went on, talking about how good it was to have people that you loved and respected on the land adjoining yours. But at last he seemed to come out of his reverie. Holding out a hand to Mary, he said, "Let me have that envelope, wife."

From somewhere Mary Carter produced an envelope tied with a purple ribbon.

Dan took it, held it, and looked at it with a smile. "Yes, sir, I like to choose my own neighbors, and that's exactly what I've done." He shifted uneasily and looked about the room. "I've also got a bad habit of meddling. I call it my spiritual gift—meddling." A laugh went around the table, but Dan held up his hand. "No, it's true enough. I'm confessing all my faults tonight. I want my own way, and I'm a meddler."

"I never thought of you as that kind of a man, Dan," Nelson said.

"Well, you're about to find out different. Here!" He thrust the envelope into Nelson's hands.

"What's this?"

"Take the ribbon off and look at it. You'll find out what a meddler I am."

Nelson looked with astonishment at Eileen, who appeared as mystified as he was.

As he undid the bow, Dan said hastily, "Now, Nelson, you've got to look on this as sort of a combination of my stubbornness *and* a wedding present for you and Eileen."

"A wedding present?" Nelson Majors took a paper out of the envelope. He stared at it and then froze into the stillness of a statue.

In the silence, Jeff said, "What is it, Pa?"

"It's the mortgage on our old place." He turned to face Dan. "What does this mean?"

"It means that the Joneses couldn't handle that farm. It was gonna be foreclosed on, so I just did a little foreclosin' of my own. I fixed it up with Dave at the bank, and I made the down payment—and that's the wedding present."

In the hubbub of talk that arose, Tom said, "What does it mean, Pa?"

"I'll tell you what it means," Dan said. "It means that place is the Majors place. That's all it was ever meant to be anyhow. The war came along and got us all kind of off track. I sort of look at the Joneses as caretakers while you boys was gone. Not very good caretakers," he added with a shrug, "but they're leavin' for Carolina now. And you can move back into your home, Nelson, you and your family. It's yours if you can hang onto it and make the payments."

And then all the Majorses were up and hugging each other, and most of the Carter and Majors women were crying.

There was quite a bit of kissing going on too, and Jeff saw to it that he kissed not only Mrs. Carter and Sarah but Leah as well. As she stared at him, he said, "That's just because I feel so grateful to you, Leah."

"You're a fibber, Jeff! You didn't kiss me because of that!"

"Yeah, I guess I am a fibber." He shrugged. But then he grinned and said, "But it's going to be just like it used to be, isn't it?"

"Almost, Jeff. Almost."

It was a night that none of them would ever forget.

When the newlyweds were gone and it came time for the others to leave, Nelson Majors gave his old friend Dan another hug.

The frail, older man wheezed as Nelson released him. "Well, you don't have to half kill a fella," he said. He put out his hand and smiled. "Nothing has ever pleased me much more than this, Nelson—that we'll be neighbors again."

As the Majorses rode home in their carriage, a strange silence enveloped them for a while. "I just can't believe it," Nelson finally said. "It's like something out of a storybook."

"No," Eileen said, "it's like something God would do for us."

"You're right, Eileen, and we'll never forget it. Not if we live to be a hundred."

She leaned close and whispered, "Now our baby will be born in our own home."

14

A New Generation

The day that Nelson Majors and his family moved back onto the old home place was one of those never-to-be-forgotten times.

The neighbors cleaned up the house and yard, then they helped move in the furniture the family had brought from Virginia—along with contributions of their own. Not all the neighbors were Southern sympathizers, either. Many had been strongly Union, but they came anyway in an attempt to heal the wound that still tore the nation apart in some places.

The Majorses endured the overwhelming goodwill of their neighbors for a whole day. One of them had brought half a steer, and a huge barbecue was prepared. Afterward there was square dancing on the grass to the tune of fiddles, guitars, and dulcimer.

"Come on, Jeff, let's dance."

"You know I don't dance too well."

"You do better than you did that time before the war—the first dance we ever went to." Leah giggled. "You walked all over my feet!"

The music began picking out another melody, and soon the two were whirling around the grass.

"I think it's nice you're so tall," Leah said, "since I'm tall too. It's hard to find a man to look up to."

"Maybe I can get some high-heeled boots so you can look up even farther."

"No, this is just right!" They went around the grass a few times, and Leah said with surprise, "You're a *much* better dancer now than you were when you were fifteen!"

"Well, I've had a little practice. Remember those fancy balls in Richmond at Lucy's house?"

A twinge of jealousy went through Leah, but she put it aside. "Yes, I remember, but that's all gone. I was really awful about Lucy, wasn't I?"

"I suppose you were, but I was pretty awful myself. I thought for a while back there you were going to fall in love with Ezra Payne."

They continued waltzing, and finally Leah looked across and saw Sarah and Tom. "Look, Tom said he'd never dance, but he does very well."

"He's going to do everything well," Jeff said. "He set out to plow the other day, and he plowed as straight a furrow as he ever did. He can't last quite as long at it, of course, but just give him time."

Three days after the moving in, Charlene and Rosie were married in the same church where the other weddings had taken place.

As they came out of the church, Eileen, who had not wanted to come at all because she was so uncomfortable and felt so poorly, said suddenly, "I think we'd better go home, Nelson."

Quickly Nelson looked at her.

"I think it's time."

Eileen was right, and on June 15 at 6:30 in the morning, Stonewall Jackson Majors came into the world.

Nelson, holding the red-faced infant, who was screaming with a powerful set of lungs, looked down and smiled.

"I think he's going to be an evangelist, sweet-heart," he said. He sat down beside the bed.

"He's got black hair like you. I hope he has black eyes too."

"Oh, I hope not!" Nelson said in alarm. "I don't want him to be like me! I hope he looks like you."

"We'll have a little girl, and she can look like me."

Nelson bent over and kissed her. "Yes, that's what we'll do."

15
Just Like in the Storybooks

Two weeks after the birth of Stonewall Jackson Majors, Jeff called at Leah's house at dawn. She was probably still asleep, he thought, so he threw pebbles at her window.

She opened the window and said, "Jeff Majors, what are you doing here at this hour?"

"Going fishing! You want to go?"

"No!" Then she abruptly changed her mind. "I mean—yes. Let me get some fishing clothes on."

Jeff looked for night crawlers while Leah was getting dressed. When she came out wearing a disreputable-looking pair of overalls, he said, "You look lovely, Miss Carter."

"Oh, hush! Who wants to dress up to go fishing? Have you got enough night crawlers?"

"I guess so. Come on. I want to get to the river before it gets hot."

They made their way along the familiar path through the deep woods, emerging at the riverbank.

"We'll go down past the big elm where I caught the big bass. You remember? The one that had three hooks in his mouth."

"I remember. He must've been a tough one to break away three times."

"He didn't know who he was dealing with *that* time." Jeff winked at her. "But he knows now. If I remember right, he made mighty good eating."

The morning was cool, and the wind sighed overhead in the trees as they followed the path along the river. They saw no one except a big dog fox that appeared suddenly, looked at them, then trotted off without any concern.

"I bet he's gotten many a chicken off of us," Jeff said.

"But he's beautiful, isn't he?"

"Yep. Have you ever noticed that male foxes are so much prettier than female foxes?" Jeff kept a straight face. "It's always that way. Male peacocks pretty, females not much to look at. I wonder why it is that males are always better-looking than females?"

"I ought to crown you!" Leah said. She rapped him on the head with her cane pole.

"Ow! Watch what you're doing! You want me to fall in the river?"

"You need it! You need a good baptizing!"

They teased each other until they got to their favorite spot underneath a huge tree. Soon they were sitting on the bank, watching their corks bob up and down with the current. From time to time one of them would catch a fish, mostly small ones, but neither of them really cared.

After a silence, Jeff said, "You know, I dreamed about this a million times while I was in the army."

"Did you, Jeff?"

"Sure did. There were times at Gettysburg and Antietam when I would have given just about anything to have been pulled out of there and plumped down beside you on this bank, catching fish."

Leah smiled at him. She pushed her hair back with her free hand, and it cascaded over her shoulders.

Jeff said impulsively, "You have the prettiest hair of any girl I ever saw."

"Do I, Jeff?"

"Sure do."

Again they sat quietly for a long time. By mid-morning they had caught a respectable string of small bass and large punkinseed perch. They broke open the picnic lunch.

"It's too early to go back," Jeff said after they'd eaten. "I'll have to go to work if I do."

"So will I." But she stood up.

Jeff stood beside her tentatively.

"I know what!" she said. "Let's go see if we can catch ol' Napoleon."

Jeff grinned. "We've tried that often enough, but I'm game if you are!"

Quickly they gathered the fish and wound up their lines. Then they walked back to the brook that flowed close to the Carter home place. A small bridge arched the stream, and they stood on it, fishing over the rail.

Leah delighted in pointing out different forms of life in the clear waters below, including frogs, crawdads, and small fish.

It was turning hot now. The sun beat down, warming their backs. Both wore straw hats, for which they were grateful.

Jeff put out all the line he had and let it drift slowly away from him. "Right over by those lily pads. That's where he likes to lie around and wait for a nice juicy worm. Come on, Napoleon, let's see a little action here!"

Quietness seemed almost a solid thing as they waited. Far away a dog howled faintly, as though he had treed a coon. Overhead a flock of noisy, quarrelsome blackbirds beat their way across the sky, headed for a cornfield, no doubt.

They stood elbow to elbow, and suddenly Jeff put his left arm around Leah's waist.

Startled, she looked down at his hand and then swiveled her head to look at him. "What are you doing?"

"Nothing!"

Leah studied him, and a smile plucked at her lips. "I think you *are* doing something. I think you're putting your arm around me."

"I was afraid you were getting tired. I'm helping you stand up," Jeff said blandly. He kept his eyes on the cork but pulled her closer. "After all, women are weaker than men. We have to be sure that you're taken care of."

"You can take care of me without hugging me!"

"Hugging? I'm not hugging!"

"Of course you're hugging! You think I don't know when a boy's hugging me?"

Jeff suddenly turned to face her. He pulled her toward him and said, "I'll show you what huggin' is, woman!" Holding her so that her face was only a few inches from his, he said, "Now, this is hugging! Do you see the difference?"

"Let me go!"

Jeff said, "I can't."

"What do you mean, you can't?" She shoved at him, but his strong arm held her tight. "What do you mean, you can't? Let me go, Jeff!"

"I've got a cramp in my arm. It's locked. It won't open."

Leah laughed. "I believe you've lost your mind."

"It's just that having a pretty girl like you this close, a fellow is—*hey!*"

124

The pole held loosely in Jeff's right hand was nearly jerked free as something hit the end of the line. He released Leah and seized the pole with both hands. "It's him!" he cried at the top of his lungs. "It's ol' Napoleon!"

"Get over to the bank, Jeff! You can't lift him out of the water here!"

"Don't tell me how to catch a fish! I caught him once, didn't I?"

But Jeff worked his way over the small bridge and then down the bank, as Leah followed. The pole was bent almost double, and several times he was afraid it would snap. He worked the fish for five minutes. Leah kept calling encouragement.

"I wish I'd brought a heavier pole and line," he groaned. "We're never going to get him in. He'll either break the line or snap the pole."

Jeff had to wade out in water up to his belt, but he finally wore the fish down. Backing up, he said, "I'm going to try and pull him in! Step on him if he tries to flop back!"

"All right, Jeff!"

Slowly he backed up to the bank. The huge fish was still struggling. "Here he comes!" he yelled. Reaching down, he stuck his hand inside the fish's jaw, clamped his fingers together, and with one mighty heave threw it over his head. "Catch him, Leah!"

The fish struck Leah in the stomach. She said, "*Whoof!*" and fell over backwards.

The fish flopped madly, trying to get back into the water.

Jeff, afraid he would lose the fish, threw himself down on top of it. "We got him! We got ol' Napoleon!" he hollered.

Leah was looking down at the front of her overalls, smeared with the green moss that had clung to the fish.

Jeff held up Napoleon. "Look at that! He must weigh ten pounds if he weighs an ounce. He's bigger than he was the last time we caught him."

But Leah was watching Jeff, and a smile came to her face. His eyes were alight, and he had lost his hat in the struggle. His black hair was in front of his eyes. She said, "If I live to be ninety, I'll still remember you holding that fish, Jeff."

He stood up, then looked at her thoughtfully. "So will I, Leah." He looked back at the fish and then took a step toward the stream.

"What are you doing?"

"I'm turning him loose. I wouldn't feel right eating ol' Napoleon. I'd feel like a cannibal."

"Good!" Leah cried.

She watched as Jeff carefully removed the hook, then placed the fish in the water. There was a sudden boiling of the creek, and he cried, "There he goes! Go on, boy! Live to be a hundred!"

He watched the fish disappear, then came back to stand beside her. "I dreamed about that too," he said.

"I'm glad you let him go, Jeff," she said softly.

They stood there for a moment, still thrilled by the excitement of catching the large fish. Leah said suddenly, "Jeff, show me again the difference between hugging and whatever it was you did."

He grinned. "You haven't changed a bit! Yes, you have! The little girl I knew would never ask a man to hug her." He pulled her close. "Leah, I wanted to wait for a real romantic night, but I guess I can't wait."

"Can't you, Jeff?"

Jeff looked down into her face, admiring again the beauty of her expression and the smoothness of her skin. "I guess I've got to tell you that I love you. Maybe I have for a long time. Since you were a little girl—but it's different now."

He kissed her, and when Jeff lifted his head, he said, "I want you to marry me. I want us to live together until I'm an old man and have to use a cane and you've got white hair. I want us to have kids and grandkids and—"

"Give me a chance to say yes, will you!" Leah cried.

Jeff held her tightly. "It'll be a while yet, but sooner or later I'll see you walk down the aisle of that little church. You'll be wearing a white dress, and I'll be standing there waiting, and then the preacher will say, 'Will you have this woman, Leah, to be your wedded wife?' and I'll say yes."

"And then he'll ask me, 'Will you have Jeff to be your wedded husband?' and I'll say yes."

"I guess we'd better go home now. We can't get married here at the river. Someday, though."

Leah said, "Yes, Jeff, someday."

Holding hands, they made their way up the creekside path toward the house. The birds overhead suddenly seemed to sing more loudly. Jeff and Leah looked up and smiled.

The Bonnets and Bugles Series includes:

- Drummer Boy at Bull Run—#1
- Yankee Belles in Dixie—#2
- The Secret of Richmond Manor—#3
- The Soldier Boy's Discovery—#4
- Blockade Runner—#5
- The Gallant Boys of Gettysburg—#6
- The Battle of Lookout Mountain—#7
- Encounter at Cold Harbor—#8
- Fire over Atlanta—#9
- Bring the Boys Home—#10

Moody Press, a ministry of the Moody Bible Institute,
is designed for education, evangelization, and edification.
If we may assist you in knowing more about Christ
and the Christian life, please write us without obligation:
Moody Press, c/o MLM, Chicago, Illinois 60610.